WHAT
LIES
WITHIN

A COLLECTION OF STORIES

WHAT LIES WITHIN

A COLLECTION OF STORIES

TOM
GETHING

 THE TACITURN PRESS
An Independent Publisher of Few Words

PUBLISHED BY THE TACITURN PRESS

http://tomgething.wordpress.com

ISBN: 978-0-9854804-3-1

WLW.PB.2025.09.02

Several stories in this collection originally appeared in the following publications: "What Lies Within" in *Soundings Review*; "Sabotage" in *The Barcelona Review*; "The Confession of Alan Watts" in *The Artificial Selection Project*.

Cover Design: Elizabeth Gething

Manufactured in the United States of America

Once again, for Janet,
and in memory of my parents

CONTENTS

PREFACE

I considered naming this collection *Done & Gone* because the stories were written years ago and, although I made a recent effort to spruce them up, they are truly creatures of the past.

The earliest story was written with all the earnestness and experience of a twenty-year-old in 1974 and the last around 2014. I'll let you figure out which is which. There's no unifying theme to the collection; they're just stories that for one reason or another I wanted to write. Though, as I edited them, I did notice one commonality: they contain far too many literary references. I blame that on my parents, especially my mother, who raised us to read and love books.

After my mother died in 2009, my siblings and I gathered to sort through her possessions, including her books. The house was filled with them, books on every shelf in every room—far more, it seemed, than the five of us could ever make room for. We did our best, taking the most meaningful ones home with us. But still there were too many.

As we boxed them up, a flood of childhood memories associated with titles and covers brought smiles and tears. The books were an accumulation of decades. Most had been lugged from Milwaukee to Tucson, back to Milwaukee and back again to Tucson. Before that, many had traveled from Boston, New York, Washington, D.C., Baltimore, and Nottingham. Some were signed by the author; some, as inscriptions revealed, were gifts from friends or relatives. Some were our grandfather's—awards he won at school; others were our grandmother's—mostly genteel novels about the antebellum South. A few held tender notes of affection from our mother to our father before they were married. Others still contained delicate annotations at key passages or showed dog-eared pages where a reader had paused.

When the estate-sale manager came to the house, he looked at all the books and said he'd take the ones with nice bindings, especially any vintage sets. People buy them because they look good on the shelf, he explained. My mother must have been churning in her urn as he indicated the calf-bound set of George Eliot and the gilded Galsworthy. The rest, he said, would go to used-book wholesalers.

Bristling at the thought of *our* books being sold by the decorative yard, I started giving them away. A young man removing furniture for the estate sale took the two-volume biography of Dickens because he was acting in a play about him. Consuela, my mother's caretaker, asked for the prayer books. A sweet older sales clerk in a native-arts store mentioned she loved poetry, so the next day she received a stack of my mother's favorite anthologies.

There were still plenty of books for the wholesalers: popular novels of yesteryear, outdated histories of the British Empire, large full-color art books, overviews of Western philosophy, and dense unread tracts of religious exegesis.

Gradually the house was emptied, and with each removal I felt the spirits of my parents and our lives with them dim. Gone were the children's classics my mother peddled as summer reading (at the rate of 25 cents each). Gone, the bestsellers passed from hand to hand. Gone, the books discussed over dinner, speed-read for school or consumed in slow motion while on vacation "up north." Those musty artifacts had charted our lives and enriched our home; the bare walls told no tales.

WHAT LIES WITHIN

"See it, the red handle?"

"This?"

"Right. Now turn it clockwise."

Martha turned the valve, closing it.

"Got it? You need to turn it tight."

"I think so."

"Good. Now open it again. Turn it all the way open then a quarter turn back. That way the valve won't freeze up."

"Okay."

She got down from the aluminum stepladder he was holding as if to steady it for her. She folded the ladder and leaned it against the wall. Then she wiped her hands with three quick pats. He nodded.

"So that's where you shut the water off. If you ever have a broken line or a leak, just shut it off and call a plumber. No need to panic."

"Right," she said, making a note on a yellow legal pad.

"What's next?"

"The circuit breakers."

"Okay. Let's do that later."

"You feeling all right?"

"Fine. Just hungry for a change."

"I'll make some lunch. What would you like?"

"I don't know. Nothing sounds good. Maybe I'm just tired."

"Well, let's go upstairs."

They climbed the narrow stairway from the basement to the kitchen, she following behind her husband, carefully watching as he took each deliberate step, his head bent, his right hand gripping the handrail.

Sunlight streamed through the south window above the sink, illuminating a cluster of amber plastic containers on the counter. A bright shaft of light angled across the brick-colored linoleum and the appliances in the room glowed.

They sat down at the small kitchen table in an alcove that looked out at Elliott Bay, Alki Point and beyond to Puget Sound. Broken clouds raced across the September sky. A white ferry, luminous in the sunlight, was crossing the choppy blue water to Bainbridge Island.

"It's turned into a lovely day," she said. "I didn't think it would."

"Yes, it has." He sat at the table but didn't look up. His mouth hung open and he was still catching his breath from climbing the stairs.

"It's nearly noon."

Without asking she went to the sink and poured him a glass of water and opened a green plastic pill case with seven slots and the initial of the day of the week on the lid above each slot. There was a clear case for the morning and a blue one for the evening upstairs.

"Maybe I'll have a cheeseburger," he said, swallowing the large yellow capsule she handed him. He took a sip of water.

"And a thick chocolate shake." He swallowed a brown one and took another sip.

"Mmm...delicious!"

She smiled.

"You're supposed to chew your food."

He gave her a wry smile. She stared back. Everything about his face had changed in the last three months. He was paler and thinner. The beard he was growing to avoid having to shave was wispy, gray and patchy, and augmented the thinness of his face. Only the eyes were the same, those of the man she fell in love with thirty-eight years before. The irises were the same determined blue with flecks of dark gray near the pupils.

"I can't believe that in all these years you didn't know where the shut-off valve was! What would you have done if it had gone bad while I was at work?"

"How many times have you had to shut it off?"

He thought for a second. "Never that I can think of."

"There you go."

He laughed, a sound like a dry cough. "There I go."

"Ready for dessert?"

He took the white pill from her hand and swallowed it with a gulp of water.

"I still think we should've sold this place. Taken our money and run."

"No—"

"It's a lot to keep up."

"We've been over this, Chuck."

"All right. So...let's go over the list. I keep thinking we're forgetting something." He looked out the window as if he could see the list, his list, better that way. "So, we did the water valve."

"Done."

"Circuit breakers next, right?"

"Right."

"Safe deposit box?"

"Check."

"Earthquake valve on the gas meter?"

"Check."

"Furnace filters?"

"Check."

"Thermostat?"

"Yep."

He paused as if the list in his mind was getting harder to read.

"And don't forget, if anything goes wrong with the car, take it to Jerry first, not the dealer!"

"Right." She could feel his eyes on her as she wrote it down.

"Ever wish we'd had kids?"

She felt herself flush, even now, and felt all the more silly for flushing.

"Mean so we could depend on them for things like this?"

He laughed. "Fat chance, huh?"

"Fat chance."

"Still, sometimes I wish we'd had them."

She couldn't look at him just then. She carefully finished the note on the tablet.

"Well, it's too late now, buster!"

He laughed again. "It sure is."

"I didn't mean it that way."

"I know."

He smiled. Flustered by the directness of his gaze, she looked away.

"You should have some lunch yourself," he said.

"I'm not hungry either. Want some more water?"

He shook his head. "Let's go do the circuit breakers then. They're out in the garage."

She repeated the words as she wrote them down: "In garage." She tapped the point of the pen on the pad when she was finished and smiled. "Okay."

"Let's go." He stood up and paused to gain his balance.

They went back down the basement stairs to the landing and then through a door into the garage.

"It's that gray box," he said, pointing with his aluminum cane to the back wall. "It's easy. Let me show you. But you'll need a flashlight if the power's out."

"No kidding!"

"Maybe I should get one of those rechargeable ones and set it up by the door. Write that down, will you?"

That evening she packed the car and early the next morning, while he washed and gathered his medicines, she placed sandwiches in a cooler, knowing full well he was unlikely to want them. As an afterthought she went into the backyard and picked two apples from the dwarf tree he had planted for her years ago. "Her orchard," he called it.

In a reversal of roles they were becoming accustomed to, she drove and he sat in the passenger seat. They headed south from Seattle toward Ashland. It was an eight-hour drive, but they had their favorite places to stop along the way.

"Have we got the tickets?" he asked.

"They'll be at will-call."

"What are we seeing again?"

"*A Midsummer Night's Dream* tomorrow and an Ibsen on Sunday. I forget which one."

"Seems like they've done every Ibsen and then some."

She nodded.

With his cane between his legs, he dozed off from time to time, his head gradually tilting back against the headrest until he lurched awake. Other times he looked out at the interstate and dry yellow hills. They drove that way for quite some time, comfortable in the silence, she in her thoughts, he in his, with nothing but the lapping rhythm of the tires on the worn concrete roadway.

"Tire rotation. That should be on the list. Every six months is the way I remember it. Jerry charges but it's easier than going to Les Schwab. I have him change the oil at the same time."

She kept her eyes on the road, unable or unwilling to go down his road. "We'll add it," she said lightly, as one might to a child. She had hoped this trip would be an escape from his illness, but his obsession with the list told her that no matter how hard she tried to pretend, no matter how hard he tried to have a good time, the weight of it was with him, with them, at all times.

It was nearly six in the evening when they arrived in Ashland and they were both exhausted. They pulled up to the modest redbrick front of the Peerless, the small hotel where they always stayed. The young woman at the reception desk greeted them warmly. She took a brass key down from the wall slot and led them to Room No. 3. It was a bright room on the ground floor dressed in floral Victorian wallpaper with matching curtains of rose and lavender. In an alcove off a sitting room, twin beds nestled side by side just as they had requested; his nights had become too fitful to share a bed. The beds were dressed in matching comforters and mounded with pillows of lace and silk brocade. The sitting room was cozy with a love seat and two stuffed chairs and an odd assortment of worn books on the shelf below the draped window. The rooms smelled of lavender and rose petals as if the flowers on the wall were real.

"Lovely! Thank you," Martha said to the pretty girl as she placed their suitcase on the rack. The girl smiled and slipped from the room, gently closing the door behind her.

He collapsed into the stuffed chair, looking small against its oversized mass. She fidgeted with the suitcase, unpacking the few clothes they had brought. She removed the large toiletry bag containing his pills and rummaged for the blue pillbox.

"Time for your evening snack, Chuck."

"I'm not hungry."

"You want to be well for the play tomorrow, don't you?"

"Stop treating me like a child. Come sit down and relax."

She was still fidgeting with things.

"Martha, come here." He held out his hand as if inviting her to sit on his wasted lap. She went to him and sat on the footstool beside the chair.

"Let me look at you," he said. He sounded irritated but with his hand he brushed a strand of hair, more salt than pepper now, from her face and smiled. Tears formed in her eyes at this unexpected tenderness.

"I know, I know. I'm sorry."

He laughed softly and wiped the tear from the corner of her eye with his thumb, following the curve of her cheek down past her mouth to her chin, sending a tactile shock of recognition to her heart. There was nothing old or ill about his touch.

"Listen," he said.

She sniffled and tried to regain her composure, looking at him through blurred eyes.

"I'll be fine tomorrow. I promise. We'll go to dinner and see the play, just like always."

She nodded, but her heart felt as if it were being squeezed by an invisible hand.

"I love you, you know," he said gruffly.

They spent most of the next day in their room. They ordered tea from the girl and sat in the big stuffed chairs reading and talking.

At one point he looked up from the *Oregonian* and said, "Did you know that if I lived down here I could ask the doctor to give me some pills and put me out of my misery tonight?"

With him, with them, wherever they went, day and night. But she was stronger today and could let it in.

"I could never do that," she said, shaking her head.

"I used to think suicide was for chickens, but now I don't know. I hate being ready to go and left waiting. Knowing the pain will only get worse."

She felt a sudden panic, as if he had embraced her and was crushing the air from her lungs. "But, Chuck! Would you really be able to do that to me?"

"I don't want you sitting beside a bed worrying that I'm in pain. That's worse than death."

"But that's for me to deal with," she insisted. "That's my pain."

"No, it should be my decision, to make or not."

She searched her mind for something to say but could find nothing to counter his argument except her own selfish need.

"But doesn't the thought frighten you?"

He smiled. "You bet."

"Well, then I'm glad we don't live in Oregon."

"I guess so." He gave her a faint smile she couldn't decipher and retreated behind his newspaper. "Guess we'll both just have to tough it out when the time comes," he said through its thin wall.

Stunned, Martha sat opposite him, book in lap, feeling the full dark terror of the separate desolation that awaited her.

The hotel restaurant agreed to seat them early so they wouldn't be rushed getting to the play. The maître d' led them across the empty room to a window table. After the busboy had filled their water glasses and left them alone, he whispered across the crisp white tablecloth: "It feels like the middle of the afternoon."

"It almost is," she laughed.

"Should we ask for the blue-plate special?"

"Don't you dare!"

He ordered the broiled king salmon and she chose the scallops and a glass of white wine. He picked at his food, spending most of his energy on the mashed potatoes.

They waited in the lobby for the cab to arrive and she tipped the driver as much as the fare for the five-block trip to the outdoor theater where the festival was held. Martha waited in line for the tickets and a volunteer escorted them to their seats. They read the program while waiting for the play to begin. It was a warm September evening and the sky glowed golden above them as the sun receded behind the tall stage. People fanned themselves with programs and the lively murmur of voices swelled with expectation as the theater filled.

A trumpet fanfare from a balcony above the stage announced the play was about to begin and the crowd hushed. People hurried to their seats. After a suspense-filled pause, the stage lighting filtered to a soft lush green and Oberon and Puck began casting spells on the young lovers of ancient Athens.

Throughout the first and second acts she kept turning to see how he was doing, expecting him to tire out, but he watched raptly, laughing as the clumsy rustics rehearsed their play within the play. It was as if he had never seen it before and certainly not the half dozen times they had seen it together. At intermission, however, he turned pale and closed his eyes. A look of pain spread across his face. He leaned forward on his cane and put his head down.

"Maybe we should go back to the hotel," she said.

"No. I'll be fine."

He said it with the same stubbornness she had seen a hundred times since he started treatment, but with each defiant stand his strength was diminished. And each time she felt more helpless.

"You sure?"

"No." He breathed as if catching his breath. "Maybe you're right. Damn it!"

They got up and one of the ushers called a cab. They sat on the edge of a stone planter by the entrance and waited for the taxi. It was the same driver who had brought them there. He nodded and helped Martha settle her husband in the back seat.

By the time they were back at the hotel he said he was already feeling better. The pain in his stomach had lifted. They got the key to the room and the pretty girl at the reception desk listened sympathetically as Martha explained why they had returned so quickly.

"All lies! She's after my body," he said, gleefully embarrassing her. The girl laughed.

In the room the beds had been turned down and a plate with two homemade chocolates was sitting on an end table with a handwritten note. He read the card and his laugh was like a dry cough: "Old Waldo sure got that right!"

"What's it say?" she asked, confused. She picked up the card he had tossed onto the table. It was a quote from Emerson: "What lies behind us and what lies before us are tiny matters, compared to what lies within us."

With more sadness than dismay she realized everywhere he looked, he only saw irony in his illness now. And she could not change it.

He offered her a chocolate.

Her head felt clouded, as if it were about to burst, and she could barely comprehend what he'd said. "No thanks."

He picked up a chocolate and sniffed it.

"Mmm!"

"Don't tell me you're going to eat one."

"Maybe just a bite." He nibbled it.

"I can't believe it! Chocolate of all things!"

"Pretty darn good, too." He took another small bite then put the rest down. "I'm sorry about the play."

* * * * *

That night she got up from bed for a drink of water from the bathroom and when she came back into the room he stirred.

"Did I wake you?"

"No."

"Are you okay?" she asked, slipping back into her bed.

"I just had the most amazing dream. I was in my house...not ours, the one where I grew up. And I could see everything. The rooms, how they were laid out. The furniture. The patterns on the oriental rugs. The crack in the plaster that ran across the living room ceiling. The scratches on the banister I used to slide down. The feel of its newel in my hand. I could even smell the cold in the dust motes that rose from the worn carpet on the attic stairs. Brother! I couldn't have remembered that house like that if I'd tried, but in the dream I could see every last detail. I still can. It all just came back... Amazing!"

She didn't dare speak for fear he'd know she was crying.

"I thought you were supposed to lose your memory as you got older," he said. "Hah! Shows what these damn doctors know."

She didn't answer. But it was as if he could see her through the darkness, he in his bed, she in hers. He drew his arm from under the covers and groped for her hand until she gave it to him.

"It'll be all right, Martha. You'll be all right."

"You sure?" she asked, her voice congested and no longer able to hide the fact she was crying.

"I'm sure." He started to say something, seemed to change his mind, then said it anyway. "I've added it to the list."

And he squeezed her hand, as if she didn't already know from his voice that he was kidding.

Note: This story was written in 2006. Washington State passed its own "Death with Dignity" Act in 2009.

THE LAPSE

I have a photograph my father took before I was born of my mother and the Crowleys in their backyard. It's a small black-and-white print dated August, 1953. My mom, who looks uncomfortably pregnant, and Ginny Crowley are sitting side by side on a bench in front of a picnic table cluttered with the fixings of a barbecue. Ginny is prettier in the picture than I remember her being in real life, with lustrous dark hair and high cheekbones. She has a far-off look in her eyes and is staring at something to the right of the camera—perhaps the flowers in Mr. Jaeger's yard next door—and her mouth, heavy with lipstick, is spread in a generous smile. She is wearing a plaid wool shirt over a white blouse and her slender hands are pressed between her legs as if she were cold. To the left of the table, Mr. Crowley looms large over a kettle grill, a beer in one hand and a long-handled spatula in the other. His eyes, darkened by a prominent brow, are squinting from the smoke and his thin lips are stretched tight as if the camera caught him in mid-sentence telling an off-color joke. Jay is there too, beside his mother, a diapered toddler with feral eyes clinging to the edge of the bench.

Even without the photograph I can recall the Crowleys' home in detail. They lived in a modest Milwaukee bungalow with the rooms all on one floor, a dank unfinished basement below and a cold low-ceilinged attic tucked under a gently pitched roof above. A broad enclosed porch stretched across the front of the house and the backyard, where the picture was taken, was defined by a picket fence on one side, Mr. Jaeger's flower garden on the other and a one-car garage off an alley in back that was screened by a vine-covered trellis.

On Sundays after church we would stop by, parking our car in the alley. With a shout of hello we'd enter through the back door without even knocking. Invariably, Ginny was in the kitchen scrambling eggs or warming cinnamon rolls and the strong smell of coffee percolated into all corners of the house. I loved our ritual, mainly because of Ginny. She had a low throaty laugh that reminded me of a cartoon parrot's and a wonderful way of talking to children that made us believe we possessed unlimited potential.

While Jay and I ate cinnamon rolls, she would ask us a stream of questions, for there was no silence in Ginny's kitchen; either you were talking or she was. I remember once enthusiastically describing a book I was reading about Charles Lindbergh. She listened thoughtfully then pronounced, "I bet you'll do brave things too, Stevie. Maybe you'll become an aviator or an astronaut. Yes, I definitely think you've got it in you to do something like that." And when we were learning about archaeology in school, "Isn't it amazing! I've read there are whole cities buried in the jungles of South America just waiting to be discovered, with great mounds full of bones and gold. You know, you could be the person to find them."

Sitting at the yellow Formica table, eating my sweet roll and gazing out the window at the tame lawn and flowerbeds of Mr.

Jaeger's yard, my imagination brimmed with images of searching for ancient treasure. How could I not be disarmed and happy around Ginny Crowley?

Mr. Crowley was a different matter. He worked as a salesman at the Cadillac dealership and always had the latest shiny model in his garage. Tall and broad-shouldered, he seemed to fill an entire doorway, leaving you with a feeling of no escape. Dark-haired, dark-eyed, stern of mouth, the expression on his face warned you not to get in his way. He possessed a temper that exploded suddenly and loudly and usually at Jay, whom he referred to as Jason whenever he was angry.

Sunday brunch would start with coffee but after a cup or two the adults switched to Bloody Marys and the conversation always grew livelier. Jay and I would slip away to his disheveled room which smelled of cedar shavings and droppings from the pair of guinea pigs he kept in a cage made of two-by-fours and chicken wire. For fun we sometimes put the guinea pigs inside paper bags to see how long it took them to gnaw their way out. "Jason," Mr. Crowley would yell from the living room after hearing our silence or giggles. "Jason!" And we knew we were in trouble. "Damn it, Jason. Why don't you answer when I call you? What are you doing in there?"

I was nine and in the fourth grade when my grandmother in Boston became terminally ill. My parents made arrangements to visit her and, at first, they planned to take me along. But it was near the end of the school year and my teacher said if I missed three weeks I might have to be held back. When Ginny heard this she proposed I stay with them.

"Wouldn't you like that?" she asked me, smiling. I glanced at Mr. Crowley, sternly silent in his large stuffed chair, but nodded.

And so, on the preordained Sunday in May, my parents delivered me and a suitcase of my belongings to the Crowleys. We sat together in the living room while they talked elliptically about my grandmother's illness. As the conversation ebbed Ginny suggested that Mr. Crowley take our picture. My parents and I stood together in front of the fireplace. "Say Sears!" Mr. Crowley said, which made my parents laugh into the bright flash. We stood there awkwardly while Mr. Crowley rubbed the Polaroid against his chest and counted down until it was time to peel off the paper and apply the fixer. Then my mom bent down to hug me, my dad squeezed my shoulder, and we walked out to our car in the alley. With handshakes between the men and hugs between the women my parents said goodbye. Ginny stood beside me as I watched them drive away, then she steered me back inside.

On the coffee table was the picture Mr. Crowley had left to dry: my mom looking slim in her new red suit, my dad looking serious in gray flannels and knit tie, and me looking small and anxious in the middle. Ginny picked it up and handed it to me, then she showed me the cot they had set up for me in Jay's room.

I still held the photograph.

"Here, why don't we tape it up over your bed." She smiled, her bright red lips stretching like a rubber band. "Three weeks will be over before you know it, Stevie. I hope you'll enjoy being here. I know we'll enjoy having you. Jay's playing with some of the kids down the alley. Why don't you go find him and I'll put your things away."

Ginny was right. After an initial bout of homesickness my stay at the Crowleys went by quickly. Families, I discovered, are like countries with their own odd customs, and at the Crowleys I was like a tourist, or perhaps more like a diplomat since I had immunity from the laws that bound its citizens.

That first night, as we finished supper in the dining room, Mr. Crowley seemed to be in a jocular mood.

"Stevie, did you know it's impossible to fold a piece of paper in half eight times?"

I didn't believe him and was suspicious of a trick; Mr. Crowley had never really addressed me before.

"It's true. No matter how large or small, how thick or thin, you can't fold it eight times. Here," he said, holding out a paper napkin. "I'll give you a dollar if you can do it. Look, it's already folded twice. All you need to do is fold it six more times."

"Now, Jack—" Ginny said and smiled as if she knew the trick, if indeed it was a trick.

"Don't interfere, Ginny," he said, handing me the napkin.

Ginny shook a cigarette from her pack of Old Golds and struck a match to light it.

I took the napkin and managed six folds before the paper wouldn't stay folded anymore. Mr. Crowley laughed.

Jay said he wanted to try.

"Then go get some newspaper," Mr. Crowley said, shaking his head and laughing as Jay ran from the dining room.

Ginny cackled and said, "Oh Lordy! Here we go."

Jay came charging back with a broadsheet of newspaper. He began to fold it on the floor beside his father's chair, counting out loud. "One. Two. Three. Four." The folds were becoming more difficult as the paper grew thicker. "Five... Six..." Mr. Crowley snickered and moistened the end of an unlit cigar with his lips. Ginny, too, was smiling. Jay put one hand over the other as he tried to make the seventh fold, but the newspaper sprang back.

"Nope. That doesn't count," Mr. Crowley said, shaking his head in a cloud of blue smoke from the cigar he'd just lit.

"Sure it does," Jay insisted. He knelt on the piece of paper, trying to make an eighth fold.

"No, it doesn't. Don't be stupid, Jason."

"There! I did it!" Jay shouted, still kneeling on the paper.

"No, you haven't," Mr. Crowley said.

"I did. Look. You owe me a dollar."

"Oh, brother," Ginny said, laughing. "Jack, I think they both deserve a dollar for trying. Don't you?"

"No, I don't," Mr. Crowley said. "That wasn't the bet." He looked at the three of us squarely and shook his head.

"Jack—"

"A bet's a bet."

Ginny sighed. "Well, come along, boys. Let's go see what's on TV."

Near the end of my stay, Jay and I were lying on our beds reading comics one afternoon after school when he jumped up and whispered for me to follow him. We climbed the narrow, twisting stairway into the coldness of the attic. The dark, unfinished room smelled of musty insulation, old wiring, and mice. Boxes and trunks, pieces of broken furniture and old toys lay everywhere. Jay warned me not to go too close to the dark edges of the room where the ceiling sloped to the floor because his father had told him you could slip between the walls and never get out. He inched toward the shadows and lifted the lid of a box filled with magazines. "They're my dad's," he whispered, picking one up and opening it to a picture of a naked woman. "He has a subscription." I looked at the magazine with curiosity and confusion. My parents kept art books on the shelves of our family room, and in those I knew from exploration there were pictures of naked women, but somehow this was different. We leafed through a few more copies, giggling at the pictures, until suddenly Jay said, "We better go." We sneaked downstairs and ran into his bedroom, crashing onto his bed in wild laughter.

Ginny was in the dining room ironing. "Why don't you boys go outside," she suggested.

Jay leapt up and I followed. In the backyard we played with Jay's toy guns, shooting each other over and over in ambushes and pitched battles. At one point, to elude me, Jay ran towards Mr. Jaeger's pristine yard. He jumped over the tulip bed that bordered it and as he landed he accidentally topped one of the tulips. He rolled in the grass on the other side of the bed, laughing at what he'd done. Then he jumped up and whacked another tulip with the barrel of his rifle and watched the bloom fly into his yard. Then another, and another. Soon half of the tulips were nothing but thin green stems and the remains of their purple, red and white flowers lay scattered on both sides of the bed. Just then Mr. Jaeger came to his kitchen window and rapped on it angrily, throwing it open with a furious shove.

"Hey, you little shit!"

Jay took off up the alley with me right behind him.

That evening Mr. Crowley was in one of his scary moods. Sequestered in our bedroom, Jay and I could hear his parents arguing about the punishment to be meted out. Ginny begged for clemency but Mr. Crowley held firm. Jay was already whimpering with fear.

"Jason, Stevie," Mr. Crowley yelled. "Come here."

Heads bowed, we went into the living room together.

"Why did you do it?"

"It was an accident."

Mr. Crowley gave Jay a whack on the back of the head and I imagined it flying off like the head of a tulip.

"Don't lie to me."

"I didn't mean to," Jay said, bursting into tears.

"Jack, go easy," Ginny pleaded.

"Shut up for once, Ginny."

Mouth clenched, Ginny got up from the couch and left the room. Jay was still crying, and Mr. Crowley was glowering.

"Stevie, if you were any part of this, you're next."

I shook my head.

"Both of you, go to your room and stay there."

For the next hour we heard Ginny and Mr. Crowley yelling. Ginny was crying, then apologizing in a strained voice, saying it was all her fault. Jay put his pillow over his head and sobbed himself to sleep. I was too afraid to get up to go to the bathroom until the house was quiet and desperation forced me out of bed.

In the morning Mr. Crowley left for work early. Ginny, full of nervous chatter, fixed our breakfast as if nothing had happened. As I looked out the window at Mr. Jaeger's yard with its neat bed of green headless stalks, I wished my parents home.

About six months later, on a Friday afternoon in late November, my fifth-grade class was in the middle of a spelling bee when our principal interrupted with an announcement over the PA system: a gunman had shot and killed President Kennedy in Dallas. A hush of disbelief fell over the classroom and we were sent home early. The following Sunday at church Monsignor Wells asked the congregation to pray for our slain leader and for his family in their moment of grief. My mom stopped a tear with a gloved hand.

After church we drove to the Crowleys' and parked in the alley behind Mr. Crowley's new yellow Coupe de Ville, which was so long it jutted past the garage doorway. The brittle grapevines on the trellis rustled in the cold dry wind. The sky was a somber gray. We hurried to the back door and went inside without knocking.

"Hello!" my dad called out as we climbed the stairs from the back hall into an empty kitchen.

Ginny came running from the living room, wide-eyed and pale. Her mouth was stretched into a grimace not much different from her smile.

"Have you heard? Someone just shot Oswald. Just now. On TV!"

"No!" my parents said in unison.

But Ginny nodded. Her hand fluttered nervously toward her mouth as if looking for a cigarette then landed in her other hand.

In the living room Mr. Crowley was standing over the television, his hands thrust in his pockets.

He gave my parents a grim thin-lipped smile and shook his head. "It's hard to believe."

Without removing our coats we sat down on the couch and listened to the newscaster describe how a man had shot Lee Harvey Oswald as he passed in front of the TV cameras on his way from the county jail to the courthouse.

Ginny was hovering in the background, unable to watch but unable to leave the room either. "It's just awful," she said, her voice constricted as if she were about to cry.

"Shut up, Ginny!" Mr. Crowley yelled, swatting his hand. "They're showing it again."

A thin, tired-looking Oswald in a dark sweatshirt, handcuffed and flanked by deputies, was being escorted down a noisy crowded corridor. Oswald tilted his head and grinned as he approached the bright lights of the cameras. Suddenly, a man in a dark suit and a white cowboy hat shoved his way toward him. There was a muffled pop and Oswald slumped forward, gripping his stomach as if he'd been punched, the look of pain on his face transforming into one of shock. The camera's view jostled as the deputies wrestled with the gunman and Oswald was whisked away.

"Good lord!" my mom exclaimed.

"Right in front of all those people!" Mr. Crowley said, shaking his head again.

"Right in front of the world! Why do we allow this to happen?" Ginny asked. She fumbled with her pack of cigarettes and looked for her lighter.

"No one lets it happen," Mr. Crowley said, contempt swelling his voice.

But Ginny was visibly upset. "What do you mean, Jack? Our president is shot in front of thousands of people and then Oswald's shot right in front of us on TV. How can you say we don't let it happen?"

Mr. Crowley shook his head. "Ginny, go make us some drinks."

"It's all right, Stevie. Don't you worry. Everything will be all right," Ginny said as she started to leave the room.

Just then Jay came in from the street.

"Dad, can I have a quarter?"

"Not now, Jay."

"Jay, why don't you boys go play in your room," Ginny said.

Later, she came into Jay's room and asked if we wanted something to eat. We sat in the kitchen as she made peanut butter and jelly sandwiches. I looked out at last May's crime scene; Mr. Jaeger had wrapped his rose bushes in burlap for the winter and mounded a mulch of fallen leaves over the flowerbeds.

"Don't worry, boys," Ginny said as she scraped the sides of the jar and spread peanut butter on the bread. "We're all just upset at this terrible thing that's happened. At times like this you have to have faith that things will get better, even though it's hard." She brought the plates over to the table and rested her hand on my shoulder. "Stevie, have you ever misplaced a word? You know, where it's right there on the tip of your tongue but, for the life of you, you can't recall it? And then, sooner or later, it comes back to you. You know it will. It always does. Well, for me, that's what faith is like."

I nodded as if I understood.

Not much later we stopped going to the Crowleys'. A few weeks before Christmas Ginny telephoned near supper time. We were in our kitchen. My dad had just come home from work and was mixing a drink when the phone rang. He greeted Ginny casually and then there was a long silence. His expression grew serious and he motioned to my mother to stop what she was doing at the stove.

I could hear Ginny's voice coming over the receiver, strident, unstopping. My dad made noises of acknowledgement and finally interrupted to say he was going to put my mother on. My mom turned off the stove and came to the phone, braced for tragedy. She listened carefully for a moment then said, "No! Really, that's all? Oh, Ginny!"

Meanwhile my father went to the sink and put some water in his bourbon.

"What's happened, Dad?"

"Nothing."

"Is it Ginny?"

"Yes, now shh."

"What can we do to help?" my mother asked. "Would you like me to come over?" She listened for another moment and said, "Well, darling, let us know if there's anything we can do for you, okay? You know you can count on us for anything. Okay?"

She said goodbye and hung up the phone.

"My God!" she said.

"What's happened?" I asked.

She glanced nervously at my father. "Nothing, Stevie. Mr. Crowley's gone away, that's all." My dad shrugged at the explanation and handed her a drink.

At the time I puzzled over their reaction; Mr. Crowley going away didn't seem like such a big deal. Only years later did I learn the whole story, or as much as my parents could then remember.

The night before Ginny called, Mr. Crowley didn't come home from work. Worried, Ginny tried to trace his whereabouts but was unsuccessful. She called the police but they were unwilling to do anything until more time had elapsed.

Then, on the day before she phoned my parents, Mr. Crowley called from a pay phone in South Dakota. He'd had it, he told her.

We visited Ginny after church the next Sunday but things were very different. She talked non-stop, blaming herself for Mr. Crowley's absence. "He'll come back, I just know it," she kept repeating. She started to cry, then blew her nose and said, "It's all right, Stevie. Don't mind me." My mom sent me outside to find Jay, who was in the garage pounding nails into a board. He told me his dad had run away.

The strange thing is, about five months later–nearly a year after my stay with them–Mr. Crowley did come home just as Ginny had predicted. There was never any explanation for his absence, and still less for his return. The only evidence of the lapse was the large silver and turquoise bolo tie and ostrich cowboy boots he sported afterwards. The Cadillac was gone, however. It had broken down or he had gambled it away in Las Vegas, which was where he ended up, possibly intending to get a divorce. The details remained fuzzy. But at some point he called Ginny, who wired him money, and he came home on the bus. A year later the Crowleys sold their house and moved to Rhinelander, Ginny's hometown in northern Wisconsin. There, Mr. Crowley found a job at the Ford dealership.

At first, my parents and the Crowleys exchanged Christmas cards and the occasional phone call. There were promises to visit them if the opportunity ever came up. But in the drift of time we lost touch and, for my parents and me, they became little more than a family memory.

It's mostly Ginny I think of. Her kindness, her raucous laugh, and her bright red smile. I hope life got better for her up north, that her faith endured and happiness came back to her sooner or later, like a misplaced word. But two other memories make me wonder.

One Saturday in the fall of 1964, about six months after Mr. Crowley returned, a friend and I rode the bus downtown to the sports show in the county arena. The presidential campaign was in full swing and both parties had set up tables in the crowded and noisy corridor of the arena to hand out campaign buttons and register voters. Beside the LBJ table stood a large man wearing a straw boaters' hat with a red, white and blue band around its crown. A woman, also wearing a straw hat cocked rakishly atop a blond bun, stood beside him. As we approached, the man leaned over and whispered something in the woman's ear. Her jaw dropped and she gave him a look of mock disapproval. She poked him in the ribs and they both burst into laughter. Only when the man turned did I recognize Mr. Crowley, who was too absorbed with the woman to notice me in the crowd.

The other memory is as vivid as a scene from a movie. It must have been earlier, a Sunday shortly after Mr. Crowley's return, because everyone was pretending nothing had happened.

We are all in the kitchen: my mom setting the table, my dad mixing drinks, Mr. Crowley helping Ginny with the cooking, and Jay and I hovering like dogs waiting for food to drop. Ginny is talking non-stop about something and her voice is bright and happy. Mr. Crowley towers over the stove as he whisks eggs for scrambling. Ignoring what Ginny is saying, he turns to me and says, "Hey, Stevie, did you know you can hold an egg in your hand so it's impossible to break no matter how hard you squeeze?"

"Now, Jack," Ginny says, "don't go teasing the boys."

"I'm not," Mr. Crowley says. "Want me to show you, Stevie?"

By now though I know better.

"No thanks," I say.

But like an addict, Jay jumps into the breach. "I do, I do," he shouts. "Let me try."

Mr. Crowley grins. He takes an egg from the carton on the counter and carefully places its narrow end against the pad of his huge palm. He curls his fingers over the larger end and compresses his grip. It's hard to tell if he's really squeezing but, as if to emphasize the force being applied, his eyes narrow and his arm shakes. Then he grins and slowly opens his hand to reveal the egg is still whole.

Jay yells with glee, "Let me try! Let me!" And with a sly smile Mr. Crowley tells Jay how he should hold the egg so all the pressure goes through the point into his palm.

"Have him do it over the sink," Ginny warns as she takes the rolls from the oven.

Jay closes his hand and squeezes. A burst of yellow squirts through his fingers and across the counter. White bits of shell crumble in his gooey hand as he cries it was a trick.

But Mr. Crowley only laughs. "You didn't do it right."

At the stove, Ginny is shaking her head over the bedlam and smiling as if, like a trick of magic, her world is whole and unbreakable, too.

A
WORLD
THAT
SEEMS
UTTERLY
FAMILIAR

I.

OTTO'S LUCK

Otto Gottlieb III sits at a blackjack table in a sea of green felted gaming tables at the Stardust Hotel and Casino in Las Vegas. His elbows rest on the padded lip of the curved table and he sips a Scotch and water with no ice. The steady tinkling that fills his ears reminds him of rain. It's the sound of coins dropping, handles ratcheting, bells ringing, cards shuffling, chips stacking, dice rolling, wheels spinning, balls skipping—a sound louder than the piped-in music or the many voices subdued by the vastness of the dark, carpeted room. A spotlight overhead casts a warm pool of light on the dealer and the table, but the faces of the gamblers on the edge remain in shadow.

Otto has over $5,000 in chips stacked in front of him, a multicolored castle built from an ante of $100, and he is debating what to do next. He could quit now and use the money to replace his roof (he estimates a new roof on his modest house in Milwaukee will cost about $3,000). He would still have cash left over for something else. Maybe a girl up in his room tonight, or a new outboard motor so the kids can ski at the lake this summer, or a trip east to tour Civil War battlefields.

But he's not really the type to have a girl up to his room even though he has noticed the two obvious hookers in miniskirts idling beside the slot machines. And the 32-horsepower Evinrude has served them well enough. Besides, the kids—Terry and Liz—are in college now and seldom go to the cottage anymore. Nor is he apt to take a trip east alone, and he can't think of anyone to go along except one of the oddballs from the Milwaukee Civil War Society whose bimonthly meetings he sometimes attends. No thanks.

Instead, Otto keeps playing. He orders another drink from the cocktail waitress in the black swishing dress. When he tips her with a chip from his stack, she says, "Thanks cutie!"

But he's not a cutie. He knows that. He's a homely man with a frog-like face, a balding, pointed head and protruding ears. He is short, myopic, and has bad teeth from a habit of eating cookies for breakfast. He is fifty-one and feels much nearer to the end of his life than the beginning.

Still, there are times when he enjoys himself. Just this morning, for instance, as he and his hangover headed across the casino lobby to the ballroom where the Professional Accounting Association is meeting, a big-bottomed woman in florid stretch pants approached him and asked if he was Wally Cox. "Why, yes, I am," he said. "I knew it!" she said. "But, gosh, you look older in person." Giggling, she asked him to autograph the damp napkin wrapped around her drink.

With his index finger Otto taps the table behind his hand to indicate he wants another card. The dealer complies and Otto hits blackjack.

The dealer, a stout, broad-shouldered young man in a gold embroidered vest, is thoroughly professional and doesn't smile or comment on Otto's luck. But Otto observes how his thick neck bulges over his collar whenever he swallows, as he does now, which makes his black bowtie bob, and how his flawless pompadour of fine brown hair doesn't look quite real. The dealer turns over two more cards for the house but goes over twenty-one and another pile of chips comes Otto's way. Of the four people at the table he's the only one to win.

"Must be your lucky night," the man sitting to his right reflects. He is wearing a blue suit but no tie, and the French cuffs of his white shirt jut from his jacket sleeves. Diamond cufflinks flash in the light whenever he asks for a card. The man possessed a large stack of chips when Otto climbed onto the stool beside him, but it has dwindled almost to nothing.

Otto laughs and says it must be true—it must be his lucky night. When he laughs there is a wry expression on his chinless face and his open mouth exposes the bad teeth and a tongue stained from nicotine. Behind large horn-rimmed glasses, his quick brown eyes shine in good-humored disbelief. He knows he is not a lucky man.

Otto wonders if the dealer and the gambler next to him think he can count cards. He wishes he could. He's good at things like that, jigsaw puzzles and remembering the smallest details of insignificant Civil War battles, from Wilson's Creek to Picacho Peak. He's good at accounting, too, and knows the FASB pronouncements as if they were Hoyle's rules for bridge, which he also knows as if he wrote the book. Or the way he can recite the entire length of Kipling's "If" and Tennyson's "Charge of the Light Brigade." He has a mind for detail inherited from his father, who was a successful Milwaukee lawyer, and sharpened by the best private schools, including a degree from Yale (where his father and grandfather had gone before him).

With such a mind for facts, he wanted to be a history professor. But at his father's insistence he went into accounting instead and, after the war, joined the machine tool company where his father had been general counsel. It's too bad that now, after a hundred years in business, that same company is struggling with foreign competitors and will soon *be* history.

On some days Otto worries about that little detail too, but not tonight.

There was a time when he believed he was a lucky man. During the war, when he landed on a Liberty ship which spent most of its time going between San Francisco and Pearl Harbor. Or when he met Helen Sloan at a Milwaukee Country Club dance and she, with her bright laugh, boldly asked him to dance. Or when, a year later, she agreed to become his wife. Then, having their two kids. Even finding the house on the leafy street next door to Mary and George Clare, with their slew of kids, on one side and Meg and Roger Benz on the other seemed lucky. Helen knew Meg from school and Roger came from old Milwaukee money. They shared many interests. They owned cottages on the same lake up north and played bridge with many of the same people from Milwaukee's roster of fortune and privilege.

Five, ten, fifteen years went by without a change in Otto's luck. Then Meg Benz developed leukemia and Helen began to ignore other obligations to keep Meg company during the long afternoons following chemotherapy. She took charge, ordering about the housekeeper and the nurse, and apprised Roger of Meg's condition when he came home from work.

"Another one, honey?"

Now he is honey and Otto says yes to the waitress even though he knows he drinks too much. He should be careful. He could lose it all if he doesn't keep his wits about him. Isn't that what the casinos want—to tilt the odds in their favor through human error? Drinks on the house!

He already feels somewhat muddled but doesn't really care. The jack of hearts and the six of spades lie on the table and the dealer is looking at him, wanting to know if he's going to stay or take another card. The dealer has a face card up, too. The king of diamonds.

Otto taps the table behind his cards.

The dealer turns over the two of clubs. Eighteen. The man in the cufflinks has already folded and laughs at Otto's dilemma.

Common sense says to stay, but Otto taps the smooth green felt of the table again. His neighbor shakes his head.

The dealer turns over the two of diamonds. That's twenty, and Otto knows he should stay. But if the dealer draws another face card or an ace, Otto loses. What are the odds of turning over an ace? An impish impulse tells him it doesn't matter. Damn the torpedoes! Full speed ahead!

He taps the table again and the blank-faced dealer, as if even he is dumbstruck by Otto's decision, clarifies: "You want another card?" The bowtie bobs up and down.

"Yes, hit me," Otto says, calmly drawing on his cigarette and blinking through the smoke.

The dealer turns the card over. It's an ace. If Otto had held at twenty, the ace would have been the dealer's and he would have lost.

"Incredible!" his neighbor says. "Balls of steel!"

Otto is delighted and grins. Balls of steel are the last thing people who know him would say he had. Helen was the ballsy one, willing to chance an affair right next door. Consoling the tall, handsome, grieving Roger while Meg Benz lay sedated in the next room (or so Otto imagines it), then smoothing her skirt and coming home to prepare supper for him and the kids.

Signs that something was wrong were everywhere: her frequent absences, her silences when she was home, her recriminating tone when she did speak. Why didn't he see them? Was he fooled by his good fortune? By presumption? Otto refused to believe his luck had changed up to the day, several months after Meg's funeral, when Helen came into the living room where he was reading to say she was leaving him for Roger. "Roger?" Otto asked, shocked and confused. "Oh Otto," she said sadly, "How can you be so blind? I don't love you. I'm not sure now if I ever really did."

Mechanically, the dealer plays out the hand for the house. He draws the ten of clubs and must draw until he loses, which he does with the next card: the seven of hearts.

"Incredible!" the man beside him repeats.

Another pile of chips slides toward Otto.

Later, up in his room, Otto unties the thin waxed laces and removes his heavy wingtip shoes. They have never fit right and pinch his toes. He plops onto the king-size bed. Across the room he sees his reflection in the dark window staring back, a small frog-like man propped up by pillows on a sprawling bed.

He gets up and goes to the window. His room is on the ninth floor and the people on the sidewalk look small. The window doesn't open. Sound doesn't penetrate the thick glass; but when he places his palm against its cool surface he can feel a vibration, as if a constant wind is pressing from the outside. On the Strip below, a sea of supercharged neon, pinpricks of incandescence, and roving searchlights pulse to their own rhythms. He watches the hotel's sign blink on, off, and on again, exploding in a swirl of light like the universe at creation to form a message of hope: Play here and WIN! Above, a vague black, starless sky absorbs the light radiating from the street.

The room is quiet. Outside his door, he can hear the occasional footsteps of people walking down the long, carpeted hallway, the fidgeting with keys in locks, the murmur of voices attempting to be discreet, doors shutting.

Six thousand, two hundred and fifty bucks! In the back of his mind he is thinking about the tax implications, and if he must report it. He glances at the phone on the nightstand but it's late and, besides, he can't think of anyone to call to tell about his run of luck.

He isn't sleepy. Although he's still a little drunk he picks up the book his neighbor Mary Clare lent him after he mentioned how much he enjoyed Alan Bates and Julie Christie in *Far from the Madding Crowd*. On the flight out he read the first few chapters but he hasn't picked it up since—too many distractions. Now, he opens the *The Mayor of Casterbridge* and searches for where he left off. As he does so he tries to recall the Thomas Hardy poem he memorized in high school. Something something obstructs the sun and rain. Something something for gladness casts a moan. It bothers him that he can't recall it.

Finally, he finds his place and begins to read. It takes him a while to enter Hardy's rustic world of solitary heaths and ancient Roman roads, of furze cutters and fustian, of coincidence and calamity, but as he picks up the thread of the story his mind focuses with newfound appreciation. Enthralled by Henchard's vengeful gamble with the grain harvest, Otto reads through the dying night about a world that seems utterly familiar, yet lost and gone forever.

Standing beside her cart in the long hallway, Luisa studies the list of rooms to clean. She wheels the cart to the next room, knocks, and announces "Housekeeping." When there is no answer, she opens the door with her master key. The room is neat and still, devoid of personal effects except for a pair of black wingtips beside the bed. The bedspread is rumpled but the bed looks unslept in. "Hello?" she says again, then checks her list and reconfirms the guest has checked out.

Someone forgot a perfectly good pair of shoes!

She finds the room key on the nightstand lying on top of a hotel envelope marked "Maid Service." She tosses the key into a basket on her cart and, feeling the bulk of the envelope, opens it. She can't believe her eyes. Not singles but hundred-dollar bills! Twenty of them. She counts again in disbelief and falls onto the bed, covering her face with her hands and laughing until she's crying. After an ecstatic minute she recovers herself and begins to clean the room. As she picks up the trash can beside the desk she finds a crumpled piece of paper lying behind it on the floor—her benefactor missed.

Curious about him, she unfolds the paper and tries to decipher the scratchy writing scrawled across it, lines started, crossed out, and repeated again and again with variations until he, and now she, arrives at:

> Crass casualty obstructs the sun and rain,
> and dicing time for gladness casts a moan.
> These purblind doomsters had as readily strown
> blisses about my pilgrimage as pain.

With her limited English it doesn't make much sense. Luisa shrugs, tosses the piece of paper into the trash and places the shoes on her cart to take to the lost and found.

II.

THE
FAITHKEEPER

As the cold Milwaukee night surrenders to dawn, Mary Clare wakes from a disturbed sleep.

At four she got up to go to the bathroom, feeling her way to the toilet in the gray shadows, feeling the coldness of the tile on the soles of her feet and the chill in the air despite the radiator's gurgle and clank. At five-thirty Timmy, her youngest, tramped down the stairs to his morning paper route, and she heard the back door shut. A moment later, the spring on the warped screen door made a guttural twang as it snapped back into its frame.

She fell back to sleep once she heard the snap, into the deep, safe sleep of morning. She dreamed about Washington, D.C., the city she had known as a child, and the convent school. Her father was saying something about a speeding ticket, how Sister Madeline had intervened. Then her mother and Ina the maid were in the large white-tiled kitchen, laughing. It was sunny, and although she seemed to be invisible to the others, as if she wasn't supposed to be there or didn't even exist, she felt happy and warm from the joke, whatever the joke was. Then she woke up.

Now she hears her daughter already downstairs in the kitchen, the kettle whistling briefly. Her husband George is in the shower. She gets up and puts on her robe. It's early April but spring still feels a long way off. Easter is near and the trees seem to be waiting for proof of resurrection. Milwaukee is cold and dreary.

The dream, what she remembers of it, puts her in a reflective mood. As she descends the stairs she thinks about her mother, whom she still misses, and her father, who always terrified her. At the bottom of the stairs she turns into the narrow hallway to the kitchen. There is a smell of garbage that needs to go out. Katie, in her flannel nightgown, is sitting at the kitchen table doing her homework, drinking a cup of tea. She is an independent girl. Quick-witted and energetic, she likes to finish her homework in the morning before school. The two of them have never been close, as if they were too similar to trust one another. Mary has always felt guilty about not loving her enough.

Sometimes she thinks she wouldn't have had children if the church allowed it, or one or two at most. She always wanted to write and still harbors ideas for historical novels about the kings and queens of England and Scotland. At college she wrote the first part of a four-act play in iambic pentameter about the death of Christopher Marlowe and she often thinks of finishing it. But laundry and shopping and homework and cooking and weekend socializing get in the way. In the latest Book-of-the-Month Club flyer she read how Barbara Tuchman wrote her first book at the kitchen table of her Connecticut home, working with documents obtained from the archives of the New York public library. How did the woman find time to do the research and writing? Clearly, *she* didn't have four children.

George comes downstairs, groomed and shaved, dressed in his gray suit. As he enters the kitchen and passes by his daughter he gently squeezes her thin neck beneath the bobbed black hair.

"Dad," Katie responds without looking up. Her books and papers lie scattered on the big round table. Biology. History. Algebra—her worst subject.

He sits opposite Katie and chews the piece of toast Mary has brought him. He gulps his coffee and glances at the newspaper but is up, giving Mary a light kiss goodbye, before she can sit down to join him.

As George leaves, their middle son (the eldest is away at college) comes into the kitchen looking for breakfast.

"Take out the garbage, Ed," George says. "*Before* school."

He gives Mary a look that says, Be sure he does.

Timmy comes in through the back door and hangs his dirty canvas newspaper bag on a coat hook in the hall. With the commotion in the kitchen Mary doesn't hear the delayed snap of the screen door. Timmy peels off his coat and hat and enters the room. He is wearing a hand-me-down sweatshirt and stretch jeans that make his legs look like knobby sticks. The pants are already inches too short. His hair is matted from the stocking cap he wore on his route. His hands are gray from the newsprint but his cheeks are flushed from being outdoors.

Like an orphan out of Dickens, Mary thinks. "Wash your hands, Timmy. How many times do I have to remind you?"

Timmy puts the cereal bowl down and goes to the sink.

Thirty minutes later he is the last to leave for school. Mary stares at the pile of dishes in the sink but relishes the heaven-sent silence, at least until the phone rings or she needs to run errands.

Today she goes to the Shore-View and is rolling her cart down the frozen food aisle when she spies Zelda Meisner staring into the case of frozen vegetables. She only knows Zelda as an acquaintance, as the woman who works at the public television station where Mary volunteered briefly. Zelda intimidates her. She seems moody, artistic. She dresses differently. Today she's wearing a funereal black knit jacket over a black dress and black stockings. Like Morticia in the "Addams Family," Mary thinks, and then scolds herself for being unkind.

"Hello Zelda, how are you? Remember me? Mary Clare. We met at the station."

"I was thinking of Kafka," Zelda says.

Mary is unsure what Zelda means and covers her confusion by laughing as if she understands. She has never read Kafka and is embarrassed because she considers herself well read.

She hastens her cart up the aisle, wondering what Zelda meant, wondering how she should have responded. Thinking how pretentious Zelda is to say something like that to an acquaintance. And where did she get such an affected name anyway?

She doesn't have much time to dwell on Zelda. She needs to get home before Timmy, who refuses to eat lunch at school. A chatty young clerk helps load the groceries into the station wagon and she heads home on streets lined with tall, leafless elms. On some blocks the great overarching trees are disrupted by sections of bare gray sky. Along the sidewalks large stumps, freshly cut, with dark brown centers as if they died from the inside out, erupt from the ground where Dutch elm disease has struck. The neighborhood is being devastated; each year the streets look more naked as the village plants a variety of spindly saplings to replace the grand old elms that graced them for decades.

Mary wonders if it would be silly to pray for the elm trees. Silly or not, she does. She prays often, holding an on-going conversation with God that picks up wherever she feels like it and breaks off wherever it falls; after all, God must know what she means.

And He must forgive her bitterness. She feels guilty for her feelings—she has so little to be bitter about. Unlike her neighbor Otto Gottlieb, poor soul, whom she prays for because he's such a dear man, and because Helen's treachery hurt him so. Mary always admired Helen's brash unwillingness to compromise, but she cares for Otto more. He's a kindred soul. Nine months after their divorce, Otto still wanders over for a drink most Friday evenings. Another orphan.

They drink too much when they sit around the kitchen table talking about everything except Helen. About politics (Otto is a Republican, Mary and George Democrats), history, art, music, movies and books. They recite poems they memorized as children. They debate the facts about the reign of Richard III (Otto arguing he murdered his nephews, Mary insisting he didn't) while George mixes stronger and stronger drinks. Mary usually cooks an omelet to get something into their stomachs besides alcohol. She mixes in green onion or chives, cheese or sour cream, and ham if she has any. "*Bon appétit!*" she says, imitating Julia Child. Until Otto stumbles home in the dark on the worn path that has joined the two yards since their children were toddlers.

Perhaps she should write a novel about Richard III, she thinks as she pulls into the driveway. If he did murder his nephews, as Otto contends, it might make a better story. Maybe it should be a detective story that proves he wasn't the murderer. Mary imagines the exchequer or the privy councilor as the protagonist investigating the crime. Plot twists churn in her mind. She carries in the groceries. Timmy is already in the kitchen making a peanut butter and jelly sandwich.

"Pour yourself some milk and I'll finish that for you," she says, her ambitions deflating. "I was going to make you a grilled cheese sandwich."

"I'm fine."

"How's school?"

"Fine."

"What did you learn this morning?"

"Nothing."

She puts the plate on the table in front of him. "I bet Sister Clotilde doesn't say that."

"We read about General Wolfe."

"Oh? What about him?"

"Nothing much. That he captured Quebec and died."

"Did she tell you how they scaled the cliffs at night?"

"Yeah."

"You know, when I was twelve I went to Quebec with my mother over Easter. I'll never forget how cold it was! We stayed at the Chateau Frontenac, right in the heart of the city. Our window looked out on the Plains of Abraham. I read *Shadows on the Rock*. It's a wonderful story! You should read it."

"Why?"

"Because it's all about Canada during those years. Don't you care about the voyageurs and the trappers and the Indians? I thought you liked history."

Timmy's leg fidgets under the table throughout this conversation. Sometimes Mary believes that if she could only make her children see the wonder of things they might become as excited as she. If only she could get them to read more. But her enthusiasm never seems to catch on; it's as if they are from another world. At their age she read all kinds of books. Her mother gave her sets of Jane Austen and Charles Dickens as Christmas presents. She devoured Kipling and Barrie, Stevenson and Chesterton. Only Katie, of all her children, seems the least bit interested in reading. Mary can't understand it. She never has enough time to read and usually has two or three books going at once.

While Timmy eats his lunch she puts away the groceries and then opens *The French Lieutenant's Woman*, which so many of her friends have raved about. But she doesn't particularly like it; she's not sure why. There's something false, something self-conscious about it. She doesn't like the way the author keeps inserting himself. Despite all of the comparisons, Fowles isn't another Hardy—her wistful agnostic—whose quaint, sad stories she loves. She turns a page and nibbles at her lunch of cottage cheese with chives and sliced apple (she's watching her weight). No, I just don't care for this, she concludes.

Timmy slides off his chair and goes upstairs to his room before heading back to school. She should put a load of laundry in the washer but dreads going down to the dismal basement where the clothes pile up. It's an endless stream of clothes coming down the chute. Then there's the folding and ironing that follow the washing. Until the age of eighteen, when she went to college in New York and lived in a dormitory, she had never done a load of laundry. In Washington the maids always did it. Early in her marriage she had not minded the chore; it was almost romantic. But that was before the kids added tenfold to the toil.

Life is never what you think it's going to be, she thinks. It's laundry instead of writing, a house in the suburbs of Milwaukee instead of...what? What had she expected her life to become? George works hard but will never earn the money her father made as a corporate lawyer. He's not cunning or ambitious enough, thank goodness. He possesses an engineer's mindset, precise and habitual, as certain as the force of gravity. She always said she married him because she could trust him. But sometimes trust feels like predictability, or safety. Or disappointment. A terrible word and yet, if there were one word to sum up her life, might that be it—disappointment? Where was her faith?

She closes the book, marking her place with a slip of paper. Braving the drudgery, she descends to the basement and loads the washer with whites. What is that quote she learned in college? "*Credo quia absurdum est.*" Was that Tertullian?

George sometimes pokes fun at her faith, saying her view of religion is infantile. It's absurd to believe because it's absurd, he insists. He's a fatalist; the war made him one, he says. But even he must acknowledge a belief in fate implies design. Absurd or not.

I believe because I can't help myself, she thinks. I believe because I must.

She also believes because her mother believed and the nuns drilled belief into her. And, despite her husband's protestations, hadn't the war made the power of faith plain for everyone to see? Hadn't good triumphed over evil, even if evil was shown to be far worse than anyone imagined? She thinks of the concentration camps, of the picture book Otto Gottlieb once showed her containing photos that were too gruesome for the magazines to publish.

Of one picture in particular from Doctor Mengele's experiments: two boys, possibly a few years younger than Timmy, standing side-by-side, naked, guardedly staring into the camera with hollow, famished eyes. It was horrible to see how wasted their bodies were, the skeletal collarbones and ribs, the emaciated arms and legs, the distended bellies. Then she noticed their bony pelvises, each as smooth as a girl's—they had no genitals—and it dawned on her they were photographed not to document their starved condition but the potential of castration for ethnic cleansing.

What kind of human being could do something like that?

It is too horrific to think about, so Mary hurries from the basement as soon as the laundry is loaded into the washer. She hates the grayness of Milwaukee and wonders why they stay there, except it's where George got his first job after the war.

Sometimes the damp gray walls and small, prison-like windows of the basement, and the gray skies that compress her sinuses and give her constant headaches, and the provincial attitudes of many Milwaukeeans conspire to depress her. Life seemed so much more vibrant when she lived on the East Coast, whether it was growing up in Washington, D.C. or going to college in New York. The Midwest—the very name conveys being between things! How has it happened she has lived here longer than anywhere else?

In the kitchen, which George painted bright yellow to cheer her, the afternoon light is milky despite the color of the walls, and she shudders from the chill. She switches on the ceiling light and turns her attention to dinner. She needs to put the chicken in the oven and peel and slice the potatoes for the au gratin recipe. She prides herself on her cooking and doesn't like to feed her family meals without a little flair. Otherwise, how will the children ever know good food from bad?

She has barely finished stuffing the chicken with lemon wedges, onion and oregano when the telephone rings. It's her sister-in-law Marian: Jane Olsen has breast cancer. Gabriella Schelling is thinking about leaving her husband (she's finally figured out he's a philanderer!). We had to send Cathy's dress back for more alterations. I'm worried it won't be finished in time for the prom. Oh, did you see the news about that murder near Marquette? That was Marsha Oliphant's brother. Did you know he was a queer?

Mary is not very good at this kind of socializing. Rather than attend to what Marian is saying, she listens to the tone of voice, waiting for the right time to interject affirmations to convey her presence. She is thinking about the chicken and how long it needs to cook and what time George will be home, if Timmy said he was coming home after school, and what about Katie? Who was the exchequer during Richard III's brief reign? Was it someone famous or could she create her own character?

She still needs to iron, and did Ed take the garbage out this morning as he was told? It's nearly three-thirty and the afternoon movie she likes to watch while ironing is about to start.

"Marian, I have to go," she says. And as soon as she hangs up she worries she sounded too abrupt.

The movie is a gangster film starring Edward G. Robinson, nothing she cares to watch. She switches the channel to a rerun of the Dick Cavett Show. He is interviewing a longhaired Englishman with a goatee who turns out to be Alan Watts. Their conversation wanders from Eastern philosophy and spirituality to anxiety and phoniness in Western culture. Mary attends to the ironing. But then Alan Watts says something that catches her attention: "Faith—in life, in people, in oneself—is allowing the spontaneous to *be* spontaneous, in its own way and in its own time. Faith must be based on mutual trust.

"Trust?" asks Cavett.

"Yes. Because life and other people don't always respond as we might wish. Faith is always a gamble."

"Meaning we might be wrong about what we believe?"

"Belief is clinging to preconceptions; faith is letting go. To have faith is like trusting yourself to the water when you swim. You don't grab hold of the water, because if you do, you'll sink and drown. But if you relax, you float."

The iron steams as Mary, who is terrified of deep water, and Dick Cavett wrestle with what Alan Watts said. She bends to her task. George's shirts first, starting with the collar and the sleeves then the back and then the front. Next, his handkerchiefs. Then her blouses and skirts.

Timmy is first to return home. She hears the door shut. He comes into the sunroom with a slice of bread in his mouth and an oatmeal cookie in hand. He informs her he's going over to Mark's house and goes out again.

Mary finishes the ironing and goes into the kitchen to baste the chicken. Ed won't be home until six because of track, and Katie...it's nearly five-thirty and Katie still hasn't come home. The dank day has turned to twilight. Where is that girl? If she weren't so self-centered she could help by setting the table.

George's car pulls into the driveway and a moment later the back door opens. He greets her with a peck on the cheek. He asks if she'd like a drink and goes to the pantry to prepare himself an Old Fashioned. Timmy comes home. Ed comes home.

"Where's Katie," George asks.

"Who knows?"

George looks at his watch. "It's after six."

"I know," she responds, oozing irritation as she closes the oven door.

Dinner is ready; the kitchen windows are streaked with condensation. They sit down at the table but Mary can tell George is annoyed at Katie's tardiness. They are about to start when they hear the rumble of Stuart Graham's Pontiac Le Mans. A car door slams. Clipped footsteps cross the front porch. Katie bursts into the kitchen with breathless apologies. Her cheeks are flushed and she stammers an excuse that makes no sense. Mary looks across the table at George, as if to say, She's your daughter, too.

Dinner goes more smoothly once Katie settles into her place. The conversation is sporadic. George asks Ed how the track team is doing. Mary asks if he's met with the guidance counselor yet to discuss the SATs. Katie announces they are reading *Hiroshima* in English class. "Did you know some of the walls left standing had outlines on them of people who were vaporized? Like frozen shadows."

"Let's talk about something else," Mary says.

Katie returns a look of resentment for the rebuke, and in her daughter's clamped jaw Mary sees a determination not to be outdone. "We're dissecting frogs in biology. I removed the ovaries on mine today."

"Katie!" Mary looks to George. George asks Timmy about homework. Timmy shrugs.

"How do you like the chicken," Mary asks, still irritated but trying to control her voice. "It's a Greek recipe from *Gourmet*. What do you think?" There are vague affirmations, nods and sniffs. "I think it's a little bitter myself," she says. "Maybe less lemon would be better."

Katie pushes her chair back from the table and stands up.

"Where do you think you're going?" Mary asks.

"Out with Stuart."

Mary glances at George.

"I don't think so, young lady," he says.

"But Dad! I've done most of my homework. I can finish it tomorrow. Mom?"

"I agree with your father."

Katie's face reddens: "God, I can't believe this. Weren't you ever in love?"

"Never!" George says.

Katie storms out of the kitchen. They can hear her clomp all the way up the stairs. Her bedroom door slams shut.

Mary and George's eyes meet. George shakes his head. Timmy and Ed ask to be excused, too. Mary begins to clear plates from the table, which is supposed to be Katie's job. George brings the rest of the dishes over to the sink and cuts the remaining chicken off the bone. He laughs softly and looks up from his work with a disbelieving grin. Mary smiles but she is thinking about Katie's temper and the one brief awkward conversation they had about sex; she worries they will need to have another.

"I'll go see how the homework's coming along," George says after a while, sounding tired.

Mary loads the dishwasher. As she pours detergent into the dispenser she thinks about the firmness of George's response to Katie, the whiplash rebuttal. Despite her certainty that it was only a reflex, despite everything she knows about her husband, she hears again the sudden intensity of his voice: *"Never!"*

A fear that is more like confusion overcomes her. Did he mean it? And how would she have responded? The questions only linger a second; they are too unwarranted to be given more consideration. Her thoughts return to the chicken, if she has enough left over to make a casserole. She hears George turn on the TV in the sunroom: police sirens, gunfire.

Later, Mary undresses in the bathroom and puts on her nightgown. She brushes her teeth, washes her face and brushes her hair. She takes an aspirin from the medicine cabinet and swallows it with a sip of water. She places the empty glass on the corner of the sink and the scrape of glass against porcelain sends a chill down her spine. In the bedroom George is already asleep, snoring lightly, *Time* magazine splayed on his chest. She removes her slippers and climbs into bed. She tries to read but is unable to focus.

She suddenly feels exhausted. There are days when it seems like life is speeding along and tomorrow her children will have grown up and gone away and George will have dropped dead from a heart attack and she will be old and alone in Milwaukee with nothing to show for it. Other days she doesn't see anything ever changing: tomorrow and tomorrow and tomorrow, with Timmy going down the stairs to do his paper route and endless confrontations with Katie.

As she slides down between the sheets, she feels a momentary panic, a flutter of the heart—she will die unknown and unrecognized, as unfulfilled as her story ideas. No sooner has she felt this tremor than she reproaches herself for thinking such thoughts. She removes the magazine from George's hands, turns off the lamp and rolls onto her side. She yawns, sighs and adjusts her pillow. Staring across the darkened room, facing the open bathroom door and the gray murky shapes of the basin and tub, she starts a silent prayer. It begins as an entreaty but breaks off abruptly because she's unclear for whom she's praying or what it is she's asking God to do.

THE
CONFESSION
OF
ALAN
WATTS

I determined to kill Alan Watts not because he slept with my girlfriend but because he presented me with an existential dilemma. Let me explain.

As you read this, as you process my words, essentially you are thinking my thoughts. And if you are thinking *my* thoughts, who are you?

Before you respond, consider this: If by reading Alan Watts I become Alan Watts, and by reading this you become me, is it possible we are all Alan Watts?

Nonsense, you say. (See! I know what we are thinking.) But if you concentrate on Alan Watts your mind empties of everything else because, as Alan points out, it's impossible to think two things at once. If you are reading this–actually deciphering the meaning of these words–you can't be thinking something else. Think about it.

But don't worry. As Alan reminds us, thoughts, ideas, images and words are mere "coins" or tokens for things. They can never *be* the things they represent. They are no more real, he says, than the imaginary lines we use for latitude and longitude.

That's the beauty of Alan Watts. Through him you sense the real world behind the veil of our conventions. You see how we confuse false idols—words, objects, time, self—for reality. It's this beauty that drew me to him in the first place. It's why I became obsessed with him. And it's why I had to kill him.

I was nineteen, a college sophomore majoring in philosophy and living in Tucson (latitude 32.12°, longitude 110.93°, as if those coordinates could describe the backwater reality of Tucson in the 1970s). There, back then, getting high was "the Way" for many of my friends. But I was also seeking enlightenment, and my girlfriend Alice happened to lend me one of Alan's books. Soon I'd read everything he'd written.

Then, during spring semester, as if by karmic convergence, he came to our campus to give a public lecture. Alice and I skipped class that day, arriving at the auditorium early to snag front-row seats. We read passages to each other from Alan's books and watched the room gradually fill. After what seemed like an eternity, a woman stepped on stage to introduce the special guest. As if Alan Watts needed an introduction!

Dressed in a saffron tunic with an embroidered Nehru collar, he walked out to loud applause. Under the stage lights his mandarin's beard flashed like quicksilver as he bowed to us in namaste. He declined the offered podium and instead seated himself on a cushion on the floor. He crossed his legs, closed his eyes and began to breathe in and out deeply. After a silent minute of tingling anticipation, he launched into a low soft chant. It was the first time I'd ever heard his voice—the warm timbre, the faint English accent. As he chanted, gently rocking in rhythm with the sounds, I found myself rocking with him, absorbing his cadences as if to make them my own.

That evening Alan charmed us with the playful insights he was famous for and delighted us with his devilish sense of humor. Seeing him in that pose, hearing his voice, simply being in his presence—that was the moment he became more to me than the mere tokens of his words. He was everything I aspired to be, and I desperately wanted to meet him.

After the lecture, Alice and I waited by the stage door hoping to get his autograph and tell him how much he meant to us. But he never came out. Minutes became a half hour; my disappointment became despair.

"I guess it wasn't meant to be," I said.

"Maybe he left by another entrance," Alice said. "Wait here. I'll go see."

She disappeared around the far end of the building. Several minutes passed. I went to look for her but she was nowhere to be found. Eventually I gave up looking and went home. The next day after class I asked her what had happened.

"I met him!" she said.

"You met him?"

"He's really cool. He invited me to a party."

"And you went?" I asked, feeling hurt and betrayed.

"Wouldn't you?"

"Sure, but—" I couldn't believe she hadn't come back for me. "So, what happened?"

She smiled. "He invited me back to his hotel."

"Wait! You slept with him?"

Alice frowned at my possessive tone and I knew the answer.

"He said my eyes reminded him of the morning mist on Sausalito Bay," she said, almost spitefully. "That's where he lives, on a houseboat."

But Alice misunderstood. My jealousy didn't spring from possessiveness of her. I envied her encounter with Alan Watts. As she shared more details about the evening—what Alan said, what he did—I realized my obsession was destroying me.

Somehow his existence threatened mine. I knew then what I had to do—go to Sausalito and end the obsession.

But this was 1972, after the Summer of Love, after Altamont and Charles Manson. Surely by now Alan Watts was wary of strangers knocking on his door. In addition to being a counterculture celebrity, he was a writer and a scholar, a man of meditation. How was I to get near? I spent weeks wrestling with the problem until I remembered something Alan wrote.

Birds in the sky leave no tracks. They are of the sky in the moment, without past or future. They leave no trace of their flight or a path to follow once they have passed. All is impermanent and there is no Way. Search and you have lost it. The more you strive, the more you will fail.

So I relaxed. And sure enough, one day my professor, an owlish old Pragmatist in horn-rimmed glasses named Jack Slaughter, happened to mention he knew Alan Watts. Years before, when McCarthyism raged and anyone who even mentioned Eastern philosophy was in danger of being branded a Communist, Jack had written him a character reference. Alan, he explained, might have been deported if not for the campaign conducted by academics like him.

Without divulging my motive, I expressed my desire to meet the man whose words I had read and reread until they were my own. "Hell, if it means that much to you, I'll give you a letter of introduction," Professor Slaughter said. "I'm sure he'll see you. The guy loves an audience. Besides, he owes me for saving his transcendental ass."

I flew to San Francisco with sixty-six dollars and a backpack containing a change of clothes, a jar of Planters Peanuts and my dog-eared copy of *The Wisdom of Insecurity*. From the airport I took the bus to Sausalito, which serendipitously dropped me off across the street from a pawnshop. I went in and bought a .22 caliber pistol and a box of ammo for twenty-two dollars. I asked directions to the address at the top of Jack Slaughter's letter: The Society for Comparative Philosophy, SS Vallejo, Gate 5, Sausalito Harbor.

It was a beautiful day, the sky and water mirrored shades of blue. Walking along the waterfront I could smell the iodine of seaweed and taste the salt in the air. Seagulls cried as they glided overhead. I didn't know what to expect but I felt an adrenaline rush at the thought of meeting Alan Watts.

At Gate 5 a derelict ferryboat lay beached in muddy shallows. The windows of its clapboard wheelhouse reflected the sun like three astral eyes. At first, I thought I had the wrong address since the adjacent pier led to a modern octagonal houseboat freshly painted white. But then I saw the weathered nameplate: *VALLEJO.*

Of course! Alan Watts wouldn't live in anything ordinary.

A wide smokestack painted bright yellow towered over the wheelhouse. Multi-colored pennants on a line, the kind you see at gas station grand openings, fluttered from its guy wires. Below the wheelhouse, in front of a passenger saloon on the lower deck, pots of geraniums and hanging fuchsias formed a green enclosure for a patio table shaded by a blue umbrella.

I stepped from the springy gangway onto the deck. I heard classical music playing inside so I knew someone was home. I took Jack Slaughter's letter from my knapsack, knocked on the saloon door and shouted hello.

"Alan, can you get that? I'm not dressed," came a woman's voice from the upper deck. Another moment passed, the music stopped, soft footsteps approached, a shadowy figure wavered in the frosted glass, the door opened–

And there was Alan Watts, in a black kimono patterned with interlocking circles of silver thread. Tufts of gray chest hair protruded from beneath the kimono. His legs were bare and pink as though he had just stepped from the bath, and he wore flip-flops of woven straw. He looked older than I remembered, with more lines on his face and dark bags under his eyes as if he hadn't slept well. Otherwise, he was the same Alan Watts I had seen on stage—the pointed goatee, the prominent cheekbones and the mane of gray hair sweeping back to his shoulders.

"Yes?" Piercing gray-blue eyes.

Speechless, I handed him the letter.

"Bloody hell! I'm not being served again, am I?"

"No!"

He gave me a suspicious look and opened the letter. "Ah, Jack!"

While he read the letter I peered past him into the passenger saloon: a low-beamed room stripped of chairs, its beadboard walls painted a soothing aquamarine. Tatami mats covered the floor. On the back wall, a jolly bronze Buddha sat on a low altar adorned with white snapdragons in a jade vase. Vestiges of incense tickled my nose.

Alan folded the letter, glanced at me and at the letter again. He seemed annoyed by the intrusion but reluctant to send me away. "How is old Jack these days?... Sorry, where are my manners? Do come in."

Just then an attractive, energetic woman wearing mint green shorts and an oversized white cotton men's shirt came down the stairs from the upper deck.

"Who is it, Alan?" she asked as she fastened the buttons of the shirt.

"The student of an old acquaintance."

"Oh? How nice! Hello, I'm Jano."

She extended a small hand and smiled warmly. She was a pretty woman, considerably younger than Alan but not as young as Alice.

"We were about to have some lunch. Won't you join us?"

Alan shot her a sidelong glance.

"Thanks," I said before the offer could be rescinded.

Jano led the way outside and brushed off the canvas seat of a director's chair for me. The bay sparkled in sunshine; the potted geraniums radiated pinkness. Two places were already set at the table.

"Alan was about to make a tomato and mozzarella salad. With basil and a little balsamic vinegar. It's delightful. Fresh mozzarella's the key. We have a friend who makes his own. Sound good?"

"Yes, perfect."

Alan, who had trailed behind, dropped into a chair with silent resignation.

"You're lucky to find us here," Jano continued. "Normally we're up there—" she pointed to a hazy summit across the bay, "on Mount Tamalpais. We're only here because Alan's giving a seminar next week.... Now, let me get another place setting." She turned to go back inside.

"Yes, and darling," Alan said before she disappeared through the saloon door, "now that we have company, be a good girl and bring us some wine, will you?"

He looked at me. "Red all right?"

I nodded. I would have nodded at anything he said. It was Alan Watts after all.

Jano came back with a jug of Gallo burgundy and three glasses. She deposited these on the table then hurried back through the door. A moment later she returned with a tray of food and another plate.

With wine Alan became more loquacious, asking about my studies.

"So, what on Earth made you come all this way to see me?"

I told him I'd read all of his books and had waited to meet him in Tucson after his talk. I didn't mention Alice, or my dilemma.

"Ah, yes! I remember now. I was spirited away to a reception with the dean of liberal arts. Dreadful! Only the martinis and a few pretty coeds made it bearable." He laughed—an unexpected, full-bodied laugh that emanated from his belly.

As we sipped wine he warmed to his role as guru. His face took on more life and the puffiness around his eyes seemed to vanish. I watched him deftly slice tomatoes with a sharp kitchen knife while he simultaneously answered my questions about the notion of individuality.

"We like to draw boundaries, but think about it. If the cells of your finger are composed of atoms, each comprised of protons and neutrons with electrons circling about like happy little planets, and the same is true of the object touched, say this table," he pressed his index finger against the marbled glass top for emphasis, "where does the table begin and the finger end? At the moment of touching, are you the table? Is the table you? Is there ever a time when you, the table, and everything else in the world aren't touching, aren't one?"

The question floated in the marine air while he seasoned the tomatoes with salt and pepper and carefully overlapped each slice with a piece of the soft white cheese. Next, he sprinkled chopped basil over the whole. Then, like the Episcopalian minister he had once been, he anointed each salad with a splash of olive oil and vinegar.

"If you can't live without the air you breathe or the water you drink or the food you eat," he said as he handed me the largest portion, "how can you be separate from them or claim to be free? Free from what? Separate from what?"

Without waiting for a response, he picked up his fork and attacked his salad. He continued to riff on the nature of things, pausing only to take another bite or a sip from his glass. Except for an occasional affirmation, Jano, who had been so talkative earlier, kept quiet, as if she'd heard these ideas countless times before. Instead, she assumed stewardship of the wine, refilling our glasses so often we never had time to question if they were half empty or half full.

* * * * *

After lunch, Jano began to clear the table but Alan held onto his glass and suggested we move to the upper deck. Grabbing the jug of wine, he stood up.

"This notion of an ego is a damn hoax. A strong one, I'll admit, but a hoax nonetheless," he said as we passed through the saloon and climbed the metal stairs to the upper deck. Puffing from the climb, he opened the door to the wheelhouse. "Welcome to my sanctuary," he said with a wink.

I saw why as soon as we entered. Light flooded the room from windows on three sides. I could see the jumble of warehouses on shore, the octagonal houseboat on one side and white sailboats floating like swans at their moorings on the other. A pilot's wheel stood in the center of the room, a pair of binoculars and a red silk scarf hung from its spoked handles. Books, photos and a miscellany of mementos crammed the shelves beneath the windows. A typewriter sat on a card table shoved into the far corner.

We settled onto cushions on the floor and continued our conversation. From below came the clatter of Jano washing dishes. She came up once to bring us a bowl of fruit but quickly left.

"The trouble is, you can't get rid of this feeling of separateness by an act of will," Alan said as he cut and cored an apple with the same kitchen knife he had used to slice the tomatoes. "It's something you must arrive at...the recognition you only exist in relation to the rest of the universe, and without that relationship, you don't exist at all. A wise Hassidic rabbi once said, 'If I am I because you are you, and if you are you because I am I, then I am not I and you are not you.'"

He speared a piece of apple with the knife and offered it to me.

"See my point?"

"Sort of." But if he was he, how could *I* be he? I needed to end my dilemma but, enraptured by his voice, I wanted to hear more. Besides, the gun was in my knapsack on the deck below.

He paused, knife in the air, searching for another way to express his idea. "The more you plumb the question, 'Who am I,' the more you realize the answer is—nothing, apart from everything else."

"Why do you think it's so difficult for us to see that?"

He shrugged and smiled.

"God is the true self of the universe, but he plays hide and seek. He is you. He is I. He is this apple. You can't see him for the same reason you can't see your own eyes or bite your own teeth."

"You said that in *The Book*."

He smiled again. "I've said it many places. To discover the truth about life, the truth about God, you must let things take their course."

"Do you really believe that? What about free will? Good and evil? I mean, what if someone wanted to harm you? Surely, you'd defend yourself."

Alan took a large gulp of his wine. "If that were true, resisting wouldn't do much good, would it?"

"Why not?"

"Here, let's find out." He rose unsteadily to his feet. "Stand up," he said, tightening the sash of his kimono and smoothing its silky lapels. He handed me the knife.

"What?" I asked, baffled.

"Stab me."

I stared at him in disbelief. He smiled coolly and straightened his shoulders, watching me, waiting.

Did he know why I had come? I felt the weight of the knife in my palm and saw what was going to happen next: the knife plunging into his chest, his body falling backward from the thrust, his head hitting the edge of the table with a thud.

Stunned, he would die in a pool of blood, helplessly gasping like a fish flapping out of water or a man drowning...

Horrified, I dropped the knife before these thoughts became real. Alan laughed.

I was shaking but began to laugh too. I felt a tremendous release in my neck and shoulders.

"You knew I couldn't do it!"

"Did I?" he said softly, staring at me as if he were watching the blood pulsing through the vessels behind my eyes.

Calmly, he bent down and picked up the knife and bowl from the floor. "Excuse me," he said, "I need to use the head." With drunken care he turned and carried the objects downstairs.

I had drunk too much as well and felt frightened and dizzy. Why had I come if, as he just proved, it wasn't to kill him?

Feeling lost, my eyes searched the room for an answer—the books lining the shelves, the framed photo of a younger Alan in a dark suit with five children and a woman who wasn't Jano, another of Alan at a Grateful Dead concert with someone who might have been Timothy Leary. Then I noticed the piece of paper in the carriage of the typewriter, a page half filled with single-spaced type. I began to read.

At first, I thought it was part of a new book or essay. But there were no other pages on the table. Just the one in the typewriter, as if he'd been interrupted in the middle of its composition (by me?) and had forgotten to remove it from the carriage or left it there to finish later. As I read further, I realized it was an intimate composition, part of a letter perhaps, or a journal entry.

in my latest book. The first five chapters cover the Tao. But what next? I could go on the way I did at my last conference chanting nonsense: "Yah Ha Ho Ha! Ho La Cha Om Ha! Deg Deg Te Te..." I can ~~get away with~~ do that at a conference because people expect ~~to be~~

entertained the unexpected. But I doubt my readers are ready for such antics; those who pay hard cash for a book don't get appreciate the joke. They want the Answer...the Way...or a way out, and a full refund.

On the Tao I have repeated myself ad nauseam in book after book. Really, what more is there to say? If I accept the Tao, I must stop trying to <u>explain</u> it (the opposite of acceptance), and <u>do</u> as the Chinese poet bade: "While living be a dead man, thoroughly dead; then, whatever you do, just as you will, will be right."

But <u>feeling</u> dead isn't the same as <u>being</u> dead. If only someone would

I heard Alan say something to Jano as he passed through the galley, then the slow shuffle of his flip-flops on the stairs. Without exactly knowing why, I yanked the piece of paper from the typewriter, folded it up and stuffed it into the back pocket of my jeans. I stepped away from the table, wondering if he would notice.

"So, what are you working on now?" I dared to ask as he entered the room. He glanced over at the table, at the empty typewriter. If he noticed the page was missing, he didn't reveal it.

"Oh, lots of things. I write all the time. It's my way of getting out of the way." He smiled and opened his cupped hands as if freeing a bird, "Of letting things go."

In that instant I wondered if he had wanted me to kill him. I looked into his eyes but they were less clear now, tired and bloodshot from the wine. The puffiness had returned to the pouches underneath.

"Well, I should go. I've taken too much of your time."

Wearily, Alan nodded. He extended his hand and I took it. We looked each other in the eye and, as he gently squeezed my hand, I thought about how we were joined. Did he know I had the piece of paper in my pocket? I knew it was there, and if in that moment I was Alan Watts and he was I, then he knew it too. He released his grip and took a deep inward breath as if to muster his energy, retrieving it from wherever it had gone.

"Thank you for coming,' he said softly. "We seekers must stick together. After all, it's all we've got...like honor among thieves."

Then, with hands pressed together, he bowed in namaste.

I still have the piece of paper. Whenever I read it, I know exactly how I was going to finish my next sentence. I see the earnest young man striding up the gangway with the stolen page of my journal peeking from his back pocket like a starched white handkerchief, and I wave goodbye, happy to be rid of my self at last.

MAKING AMENDS

I was too young to deal with the celebrity that came my way in the spring of 1979. As I completed an MFA at the Iowa Writers' Workshop, my first book of poems won the prestigious Yale Series of Younger Poets prize. Shortly thereafter, I was offered a one-year gig as a writer-in-residence at the University of Arizona, with an option for a full-time teaching position the following year.

Gary Padgett, my champion at Arizona, was also young and determined to make his name. Armed with an assertive intelligence and a Ph.D. in American literature from Princeton, he was one of the first academics to sing my praises. "Rich Woodward is a young poet to watch," he wrote in an early review of my book. "His is a fresh new voice in the tradition of Lowell and Berryman, while his mystical, often hallucinatory imagery evokes the transcendental dreamscapes of Poe."

He must have meant it, because he convinced his skeptical peers to invite me to Tucson.

That August I drove to the desert with all my possessions stowed in the back of a rusted old Buick Skylark. I rented a small house near campus with a sunset view of the Tucson Mountains and a Mexican neighbor who liked to sing as she hung laundry in her backyard. To celebrate my arrival, I sold my car and bought a motorcycle, a temperamental but fast Norton Commando, along with a pair of lizard-skin Tony Lamas and a fleece-lined leather jacket.

My first day on campus Gary showed me around, introducing me to other faculty members and praising my work as we went. Toward the end of the day we left the main campus to visit the poetry center. As we crossed Speedway Boulevard and cut through an unpaved alley, Gary explained how a wealthy patron had bequeathed the modest mid-century ranch house to the university. "It may not look like much, but to my knowledge no other university has placed so much emphasis on contemporary poetry."

We came to a wooden gate in a tall weathered fence. Through the slats I glimpsed a garden and a patch of Bermuda grass.

"We have over 10,000 volumes of poetry," he said as he opened the gate. "And a dozen varieties of rose. I know that fact because my wife works here as a volunteer."

She was in the garden, bending down to clip a rose.

"Val, this is Rich Woodward, the poet I was telling you about."

She stepped gingerly from the flowerbed and wiped her bare feet in the grass. She wore a lilac tank top and a long, sheer sage-green muslin skirt. As she approached, the slanting sunlight outlined long legs through the diaphanous material. She brushed a strand of hair from her face and, after carefully transferring the rose and clippers to her left hand, took mine in a delicate grasp.

"I've already read your book. Your poems are wonderful."

"Valerie is an aspiring poet herself," Gary said.

"Oh? Then I hope you'll let me read them sometime."

"No, no, no!" she said, laughing. And as if to change the subject, she held out the rose for me to smell, a dense creamy yellow bud, its outer petals flushed with scarlet. "It's called Double Delight. You'll only get a hint now, but in the morning it smells like spices."

Later that year I wrote a poem about the old Spanish mission outside Tucson, the way you enter its cool whitewashed interior and are drawn toward the ornately carved and gilded reredos behind the altar. But turn around and you are startled by a luminous fresco of the Virgin painted above the main portal. Serene, in flowing blue robes, she floats on a cloud surrounded by cherubs with Indian faces. The poem ends, "She stills the doleful dirge/ that echoes in my heart/ for a star that's lost and losing/ to heaven's relentless drift./ Her gaze, her grace astonish—/ like a timeless promise/ like a tender caress."

When I read it to my undergraduate class, one of my more literal students hastened to point out there is no Madonna over the door at San Javier. I wrote that poem about Valerie.

She had just turned twenty-eight. Her Celtic roots were written in unruly waves of reddish blonde hair and a spray of freckles across high cheekbones. Playful blue eyes and a self-effacing smile softened a tendency to frown as she deliberated on her choice of words. She and Gary had been married three years.

Although he was friendly enough, I always found Gary, dressed in his starched Oxford-cloth shirts and gray flannels, to be somewhat aloof and patronizing. But Valerie and I were kindred souls. I sensed it from our first meeting. Like me she was an army brat. Like me she had bounced from college to college before completing her degree. We were children of the liberal arts, orphans of the sixties with vestiges of the counterculture imprinted on our souls. She was a budding feminist who walked around the poetry center barefoot and braless. I wore my hair in a ponytail and sported a bushy mustache.

Poets of that era, at least those sheltered by a university stipend, spent their days in the classroom impressing wide-eyed undergraduates with quasi-profound observations on life. Evenings were mostly spent with graduate students, drinking and bullshitting in bars. Especially single poets like me. Either you were gay, lecherous and alcoholic or you were straight, lecherous and alcoholic. I was no exception, and I wasn't gay.

I taught two workshops a week. The rest of the time I was free to write. My office was a converted bedroom in the poetry center. Valerie occupied a desk in the reading room outside my office in what had once been the living room—a bright open space with bookshelves lining the walls, two large picture windows and a sliding door leading to the garden.

Often I didn't stumble in until ten in the morning. By my sunglasses and disheveled clothes, Valerie knew whenever I was hung over. My voice rasped, and I'd sit in my office with the lights off and the blinds drawn.

"Poor Lycidas," she'd say, coming to offer me a cup of coffee and smiling as she recited Milton, whom she knew I loathed. "For Lycidas is dead, dead ere his prime." Her voice soothed even as she joked. I teased back, asking when she was going to let me read her poems. But she always demurred. "I don't feel safe with you yet," she'd say, smiling.

That first semester Valerie watched the odd stream of students come to my office for advice. One day she commented that I spent a lot more time with the coeds, especially the pretty ones. "What can I say? Poets are drawn to beauty," I replied. "That's why I want to read your poems." She shook her head and backpedaled from my office, "No sir. No way. No."

Another day she heard me raise my voice to a gangly sophomore with curly hair. The kid had written a decent poem but it still needed lots of work. I had a hangover and he was arguing, telling me how revision killed spontaneity.

"Bullshit! Poetry's hard work. It's like fucking!" I yelled, wanting to shock him into submission. I heard Valerie suppress a laugh. The kid fell silent. His ears and cheeks turned red, and it dawned on me he was probably still a virgin.

After he left, I stepped out of my office and expressed my frustration by pretending to wring his skinny neck.

Valerie laughed. "You're a dangerous man, Rich Woodward. You should be more careful." But as she chided me I registered something else in her eyes.

Our game went on like that until February, when spring came to the desert with the fragrance of roses and sweet acacia. One exceptionally slow, hot afternoon, after we'd opened all the windows and doors to no avail, I convinced her to play hooky. We locked up and rode my motorcycle to a resort in the Catalina foothills with a terrace restaurant overlooking the valley. Sunlight glinted off the windows of the buildings downtown. Further south, dust devils skipped across the valley floor, their funnels whipping into furious gyres and expiring as suddenly.

We chose a table at the edge of the patio underneath a bougainvillea-covered ramada and ordered a pitcher of sangria. The restaurant was nearly empty. Two bored waiters in white jackets huddled in private conversation near the bar. It was as if we were alone on an elevated stage. The soporific plop-plop of a tennis ball being lobbed back and forth nearby only reinforced our sense of refuge from the heat. I filled her glass and watched the beads of condensation run down the side of the pitcher.

"Now?" I asked.

"Yes, I think now."

In the flickering sunlight, as leaf shadows danced upon the tablecloth, Valerie took her notebook from her shoulder bag and with embarrassed selectivity began to read her poems.

Sparrows hopped underfoot searching for crumbs as she described mornings in her garden, her fear of death, her body's reaction to desire. She wrote of leaving places she loved and of being left behind. They were good, honest poems. I took her hand and asked her to read several again. We talked about their origins and, by the time we left, I had glimpsed the vulnerability beneath her humor and laughter.

We were both slightly drunk. Her arms hugged my waist and her body pressed against mine as we rode back. I revved the engine and we swayed through the curves as waves of heat rippled off the blacktop. Like travelers returning from a foreign land, we pulled up to the poetry center feeling confusion and regret. Her cheeks were flushed as she hopped off my bike.

"It's like flying!" she said, laughing. She came near and kissed me on the cheek. "What a lovely afternoon! Thank you for lifting me from my tiresome rut."

I reached for her hand and drew her toward me. "Thank you for trusting me with your poems. They're just like you." I leaned to kiss her but she averted my advance, turning her head so my lips grazed her cheek. We both laughed. "Still think I'm dangerous?"

"More than ever," she said, nodding.

Back then I believed in fate, in a creative force that guides our lives. I believed in star-crossed lovers and serendipity when writing a poem. And that was how I felt about Valerie. I had never met anyone I felt as close to. Maybe that's why I refused to accept she was married. I've since learned our lives are a series of accidents, a string of coincidences that ultimately break us. And if God exists, he is indifferent to our prayers or savagely cruel.

Shortly before I got sober I ran into an acquaintance from my Tucson days in the San Diego airport. He recognized me sitting at the bar while I waited for my flight to Portland. I couldn't recall his name but remembered him as a mediocre graduate student.

"Wally Sieffert," he reminded me, shaking my hand.

"That's right. How the hell are you, Wally?"

Over a beer we talked about old times, of humorous and outrageous moments in the bars on Fourth Avenue. Then he stood up to go, and as he paid his tab, he said, "By the way, did you hear about Valerie Padgett?" I gave him a sidelong glance—has she left Gary? was my first thought—and shook my head. I felt a sense of foreboding and wondered if he had somehow known about us. "She died last month. From cancer. Ovarian...or cervical...one of those. Tough for Gary, huh?" He hoisted his satchel to his shoulder. "Well, I gotta run. Take care, Rich." And with a thumbs up he rushed off, leaving me at the bar with over an hour to kill before my flight and images of Valerie flooding my head.

Nine months after joining AA I began working through a long list of amends I needed to make, until Gary's name stood alone. I wasn't sure where he lived now but knew it wasn't in Tucson. I searched online and discovered he was teaching at the University of Washington, which meant Valerie must have been there too, only three hours up the road from me when she died. I worked up various drafts of a letter but none felt right. I kept trying to imagine Gary's expression, but after all this time I could barely picture him. I decided I had to apologize in person.

But how? How do you telephone someone you last saw over thirty years ago under the shittiest circumstances and ask to see him without explaining why?

I never understood Valerie's reasons for ending our relationship or why, after she broke it off, she felt compelled to tell Gary. It was such an impetuous thing to do, but that too was just like her. Did she think her honesty would restore the integrity of their marriage? All it did was cause needless pain. Words said that shouldn't have been. Accusations. Retribution.

The last time I saw Gary was in the hallway of the English department: "Get out of my way! And don't ever cross my path again or I'll smash your fucking face." It was all he said, but he didn't need to say more. Instead, he simply made sure I wasn't offered a position the following year.

I dreaded the phone call but made it anyway. Gary answered, his voice as thin and tenuous as a cirrus cloud. I had recently turned sixty so he must have been sixty-three or four, looking downhill to retirement. Without Valerie.

"Gary, hi. It's Rich. Rich Woodward."

There was a long silence, then a discernable sigh. "Shit. What do you want?"

I heard my nervousness spill out in an unnatural staccato laugh. "How are you, Gary?"

"Christ, I thought you'd died."

He was too good a scholar not to have seen my poetry, even if my poems were less frequently published and in more obscure places than before.

"No, not dead. But I teach at a community college in Portland, which can feel a lot like hell." I hoped he'd laugh.

No acknowledgement.

"Gary, I heard about Valerie. I'm so sorry. I thought about sending you a note but didn't know where you lived or, quite frankly, what to say. Then I thought maybe it was better to leave well enough alone."

"And then as usual you didn't. Well, you've found me. What do you want?"

I didn't take his reaction personally; I'd expected initial anger. "Gary, I'd like to see you. I'll be in Seattle next week and I was hoping we could have coffee or something." The explanation seemed inadequate. "It's important to me. There are some things I need to say and they're better said in person."

Another long pause. "Gary?"

"When?"

"Next Tuesday at ten?"

"I'm teaching then."

"Okay, can you suggest a time?"

"I'm free at four."

"Fine. Four it is. Shall I come to your office?"

"No. There's a Starbucks on University Way, off 45th. Or would you prefer a bar?"

Was that another jab?

"I'm sober now, Gary. That's one of the things I want to talk to you about."

"Congratulations," he said without kindness. "How will I recognize you?"

I caught the gibe but laughed it off. "Tuesday at four then. Thanks, Gary." But he may have already hung up.

He didn't need to know I was only coming to Seattle to see him. I got there in the early afternoon and wandered around the University Bookstore until our meeting. I arrived at the Starbucks early to select a quiet table, finally settling on one beside the fireplace. I sipped a latte and watched the misting rain, wondering how to begin but trusting the words would come.

Dressed in a black wool overcoat, Gary appeared on the other side of the street, waiting at the crosswalk for the light to change. He had gained some bulk and grown more distinguished with age. The straight nose, broad brow and long sweep of gray hair gave him a dramatic, old-fashioned appearance. He crossed the street with a confident stride, looking more like a banker than an expert on Hawthorne, Melville and Poe. His face, however, was still angular, his expression as solemn as Ahab's.

He entered the coffee shop and, unbuttoning his overcoat, looked around. I waved and he came toward me. I stood up to shake his hand.

"Hello, Gary. Thanks for coming."

"Rich." Ignoring my extended hand, he removed his coat and draped it over the chair between us. He sat down opposite me.

"Can I buy you a coffee?"

He shook his head.

"You sure?"

"Yep."

"You look good, Gary. Solid."

"Hmm. You look..." He peered down his nose at me as a judge might at a recidivist: "Dry."

The caustic tone reminded me of a time early on when he and Valerie had invited me to their house for dinner. It was a clear, starlit evening and afterward we were sitting on their patio having a nightcap. Gary was talking about his research on Poe's *Eureka* when Valerie interrupted to ask what "paronomasia" meant. In that same derisive tone, he chastised her for not knowing the word and, rather than tell her its meaning, suggested she go look it up. Valerie leaned over and placed her hand on my arm: "Academics can be such pompous asses! Don't ever become one, Rich. It will kill your poetry." At the time we all laughed.

"Been a long time, hasn't it?" I said to him now.

I began by telling him about my recovery, how I'd hit bottom the year before and finally joined AA.

Gary leaned on an elbow. His hand partially obscured his mouth and his index finger tapped against his upper lip. Either he was impatient or nervous—I couldn't tell which. I had to raise my voice to be heard over the sputtering of the espresso machine.

"You know, of all the things I regret, and believe me there are plenty, Gary, the one I regret the most—something I can't forgive myself for—is what I did to you."

Gary remained quiet, waiting.

"This is really hard...I mean, with Valerie's death. I know how hard it must be for you."

Gary's head jerked back as if he'd been struck. "Do you, Rich?" His voice assumed that distant thinness I'd heard on the phone. "So you know what it's like to lose your wife of thirty-six years? Sitting by her side as she heaves her guts out. Holding her hand as she wastes away in a hospital bed. Of course! You've probably written a poem about it."

The faintest smile creased his mouth.

"I didn't mean it that way, Gary. Hell, I'm lucky to keep a relationship going for a year. Maybe if I'd been sober. I'd like to think if the right person came along..."

I was off track and wondered how to restart. I breathed in and tried again:

"Gary, about what happened. I don't mean to open old wounds but I owe you an apology. How I behaved was reprehensible. I betrayed your trust, our friendship—"

Gary swallowed a hard laugh. "Friendship! Don't kid yourself. We weren't friends, Rich. Not then, not now." He shook his head and studied his hands, which were clenched together on the table. His next words came slowly.

"You know, I was wondering why you wanted to meet. Now I'm beginning to see. So far, this whole conversation has been about you. Which shouldn't surprise me because it always was about you, wasn't it?" He looked at me and his gray eyes were clear and hard. "You showed no consideration for me, for Valerie, or for anyone else that I ever saw. Go ahead, blame it all on alcohol. But do you really expect me to say it's okay? That time heals all wounds? That I forgive you? Are you still that fucking delusional?"

I tried to tell myself it was his grief speaking, the rage at Valerie's death unleashed, and I should cut him some slack. But with so much residual anger I could no more make amends to Gary than bring Valerie back from the dead. Then the idea struck me: allowing him to vent was one small way, even if he didn't realize it.

"It's okay, Gary. Let it out."

He glared at me as if I had sworn at him.

"You arrogant, condescending–" Disgust contorted his face. "Who are you to tell me it's okay? Christ! You still don't have a clue, do you?"

I felt shame and fear rising from my belly. If I'd momentarily thought I could help this man, I was wrong. The metallic taste on my tongue warned me to protect myself.

"Look, Gary, I'm sorry. Sorry about Valerie. Sorry for you. There's not much else I can say, is there?" I felt my own anger rising. "I hoped you could accept my apology. If Valerie were alive today–"

"Well, she isn't!" Gary's hand sliced through the air to cut off further conversation. The chair legs screeched against the floor as he stood up. He grabbed his coat and, after fishing for the sleeves, hefted it onto his shoulders. He leaned across the table, towering over me, his fists pressed against its hard surface.

"And for the record, I want to correct something you said. It wasn't I who got you fired." A fleck of spit landed on my sleeve from his effort to control his voice. "Valerie asked me to but I refused. I wasn't about to compromise my integrity to mollify her bad conscience. Believe it or not, Rich, even though I hated your guts I thought you had some talent."

"Valerie?"

"What? Think she wanted you skulking around after your little affair?"

"But– Then why?"

Gary began to laugh as if he'd heard something cosmically funny.

"Rich, you were a drunk!" He shook his head and the amusement drained from his face. "Do me a favor. Don't call me again. I don't need more crap in my life." And he left.

I felt spent. The hiss of the espresso machine, the music and chatter around me were like mind-numbing static. I tried to think what my AA sponsor would say but none of his advice seemed appropriate for what had just happened. I'd been through some tough encounters since sobering up but others had been able to forgive. Not Gary. I rubbed my temples. I wanted a drink badly. Before that urge seeped any deeper into my consciousness, I stood up.

I walked through the misting rain to my car. It was dark now and the traffic leaving Seattle was backed up, a river of red lights reflecting on wet pavement. I replayed our conversation, trying to process what had gone wrong. I kept getting stuck on Gary's comment. Why would Valerie have wanted me fired? Had Gary said this to get back at me? He seemed too enmeshed in his own anger to be that malicious, that calculating. Which turned my thoughts to Valerie.

As I drove south on I-5, I recalled another afternoon several months after our ride in the foothills. Valerie and I had spent the afternoon at my place making love. It was an even hotter day and we had shared a bottle of wine. The Mexican woman next door was singing *rancheras* in a deep, throaty voice that drifted through the open window. Valerie went to shower and came out of the bathroom wrapped in my towel, her skin glistening from the steam. Hearing my neighbor's plaintive song, she placed her hand to her heart and mimed the words—*mi corazón...tu amor...el dolor...no llores*. Suddenly, she leapt astride me on the bed. Her hair was damp and smelled of shampoo as she leaned over me. She was laughing but her expression turned serious, challenging.

"You know, I'd leave him, Rich. I really would, if I knew you loved me. I'd go with you wherever you want to go." Her eyes searched mine.

Maybe it was the wine, or the suddenness of her actions, but instead of telling her the truth—how much I loved her and how much that frightened me—I laughed as if her declaration were part of the mime. Her eyes went still and her mouth set in a rigid smile. Gently, she caressed my cheek.

"I better go," she said, getting off the bed.

I regretted my deflection but didn't know how to take it back. Instead—Jesus, forgive me—I sat up and drained my glass.

THE
UFOLOGIST

Sometimes you just have to accept what you can't believe.

My dad is head of the UFO Identification Network in Tucson, Arizona. He's been the driving force—the sole force, really—behind UFOIN for years. He founded the organization and, except for a few small donations, has kept it going with his own time and money.

You might think it's just a bunch of kooks who believe in aliens and UFOs, but that's not entirely true. My dad is a Caltech graduate in mechanical engineering who worked for a number of respected defense contractors. At one time or another we lived in Las Vegas, Long Beach, Las Cruces, Phoenix, and Plano, Texas, while my dad worked on various classified projects. Sometimes the contracts ended or died for lack of funding and sometimes my dad's ideas of how a project should be run didn't mesh with his boss's.

Except for UFOIN, he worked the longest on a top-secret Air Force program in the Nevada desert where they installed high-speed mining machines in underground caverns. The idea was, if a nuclear war happened and the surface of the earth was obliterated, these machines would excavate shafts from secret locations underground so America could deliver a second strike.

My dad was so proud of that project he once took me—an eleven-year-old in braids—on a hot and difficult four-mile hike to a ridge overlooking the site so he could show me the tests they'd made. In a matter of hours, these huge machines, twenty feet in diameter, had bored through solid rock from a cavern hundreds of feet underground. They'd even piled rubble on the ground to simulate the debris from a nuclear blast, and still the machines emerged without a hitch. You could see their cutting heads sticking up from the desert floor like gigantic drill bits.

"What will they do with them now?" I asked, handing back the binoculars.

"This was only a test, honey. In a war we'd cut them up with acetylene torches. Then we'd bring up missiles from underground repositories, erect them in the silos left by the machines and send them off as a nasty little surprise for our Soviet friends."

He talked like we'd be there underground with the generals and scientists in their bunker. But, if it ever really happened, I figured we were goners, toasted in our bomb shelter at home.

Yes, thanks to my dad, we were one of the few families in the nineteen-eighties who actually had a bomb shelter. Instead of the swimming pool Mom and I wanted, my dad had buried a steel chamber in our backyard with a reinforced door. Inside was a Geiger counter and enough provisions to last a year. It just about killed him when we had to move again and the people who bought the house refused to pay anything extra for the shelter.

But the end of the Cold War put the kibosh on the Air Force project, and my dad had to look around for work again in a market glutted with defense contractors. Not to worry, he said.

After receiving his notice, he still had ninety days to document his part of the project.

That's when he saw his UFO, or, as he'd tell you, it was on Friday, January 25, 1992 at 2108 hours.

That night, after fourteen hours of work, he was driving home from the test site. The desert was cold and dark without a moon, and the stars were bright. He could see the lights of Las Vegas glowing on the horizon as he drove over the pass and descended into the valley. Then he noticed three points of light moving in unison like an isosceles triangle across the sky. He pulled to the side of the road to watch, more puzzled than anything, as the points came toward him at a steady speed.

He was about to dismiss them as an Air Force wing formation flying at high altitude. But then he realized the lights were actually on the underside of a huge black chevron-shaped object that blocked out the stars above. It looked as wide as a football field, he said.

As the object came overhead he began to hyperventilate. But as suddenly as it had appeared, the ship, or whatever it was, sped off without making a sound. At high speed, it veered right and in the blink of an eye disappeared over the crest of the mountains.

I'll never forget when my dad came home that night. He was jumping around like Richard Dreyfus in *Close Encounters of the Third Kind*, barely able to speak as he tried to tell us what he'd seen. He didn't know what to do. It was as if he'd discovered the world was really flat and no one believed him.

My mom said he was overworked and tired. He must have fallen asleep and dreamed it.

My dad got upset and said he saw what he saw. He stomped out to the backyard and kept vigil in a lawn chair for the rest of the night. The next morning he scanned the newspaper to see if anyone had reported it. Nothing. So he called some of his contacts in the Air Force and discreetly asked if they knew anything about it.

Of course, no one did. But that didn't change his mind. Irritated, Mom left for work.

"Even if they know, they aren't going to acknowledge it," he said to me.

"Why not?"

"Because. Either they're afraid we'll panic or they're too afraid to admit they aren't in control anymore."

"What do you mean?" I asked, feeling frightened.

"Honey, with technology like that, we aren't."

I could tell from the way he was talking he'd already made a mental shift. He was now a believer.

"Maybe it's the Russians," I said.

"Don't be silly, honey. They couldn't even keep up during the arms race. Besides, if it was the Russians or the Chinese or anyone else for that matter, you can bet the government would know about it. They wouldn't be canceling projects; they'd be working 24/7 to ramp up new ones."

For a long time I blamed my dad for ruining my childhood. He didn't find a new job, which was why we had to sell the house with the bomb shelter. I'd just turned thirteen, and once more we were moving. We were also running out of money, so this time we went to Tucson where my mom's parents lived. Mom and Dad moved into their guesthouse. I stayed in my grandparent's spare bedroom. The house sat on the edge of a wash that ran up into the Rincon Mountains. I'd see roadrunners and rabbits and the occasional coyote trot by. I had the swimming pool I'd always dreamed of. But the situation was hard on my parents who were fighting all the time.

Even though there wasn't much demand for mechanical engineers in Tucson, my dad assured us he'd find a job and we'd move to our own place. But the UFO thing started to get in the way. He'd go for an interview and it would be going fine. Then he'd bring up UFOs and he'd never hear back. Mom kept telling him to shut up about it, but he wouldn't. It was like he'd found religion.

When I brought home friends from school, he'd be sitting around reading books about UFO sightings and alien abductions. That was bad enough, but if I invited a friend to sleep over, he was usually out on the patio with his binoculars half the night, scanning the sky. I told my girlfriends he was into astronomy, but driving them home the next day he'd launch right into the whole thing.

"Is your dad for real?" my friends asked.

Pretty soon I stopped inviting them over and stayed at their houses whenever I could. After a year or so, my problem solved itself, but not the way I'd hoped. My parents split up.

My dad took a job managing a motel near the airport. Mom and I stayed with my grandparents. I saw him maybe once a month, usually on Saturdays when we'd go to a movie. Over lunch, he'd ask a few questions about Mom and me, and then, as if he'd run out of things to talk about, he'd launch into the latest UFO sightings. It was like he'd been abducted. I just wanted my dad back.

For me, the last straw came when I invited him to my high school graduation and he didn't show up.

"I'm so sorry, honey," he said the following week. "There was an unusual occurrence in Texas that had my phone ringing off the hook. But I'm so proud of you."

By now though I didn't much care what excuse he made.

"We're moving to Portland," I said, wanting to hurt him. "Mom's marrying Blake." Meaning her boyfriend.

Stay with me, I hoped he'd say, or, I'll miss you so much, or, I'll always love you. But he gave me a resigned look from across the table of the Denny's where we'd gone for pie.

"I know, hon," he said. "You'll like Portland."

* * * * *

I met my husband in my senior year at Portland State. Evan only met my dad for the first time at our wedding. By then my dad's UFOIN website was up and running. I tried to intervene whenever he brought up the subject in front of others, but he managed to corner Evan at the rehearsal dinner.

"No one's ever created a systematic way to track UFOs until now," my dad told him. "Now people can call the hotline or submit reports online. And people from all over the world are contacting us. We're on the verge of a major breakthrough. The evidence is mounting."

"Okay!" Evan said, smiling politely and gulping his champagne.

Evan agreed my dad was a nut case, but he couldn't understand why I didn't want anything to do with him. "He wasn't your father," I said, unable to explain all the shame and anger I felt.

When Susie was born, Evan suggested sending my dad some photos of his granddaughter. I had to think twice about it but relented. Six months later my dad sent Susie a pink Oshkosh B'gosh jumpsuit that was already too small, with a note apologizing for not mailing it sooner, saying he was terribly busy. Nothing had changed.

Except I was no longer that unhappy teenager craving his love. I determined not to let him hurt me anymore. With Susie around, I couldn't afford the wasted energy.

At least that's what I told myself. Then Evan showed me an article in the events section of the *Oregonian*. McMinnville was holding its annual UFO Festival in two weeks and my dad was the keynote speaker. The fact he didn't let me know he was coming up to the area told me how estranged we had become, and I felt pretty awful. Evan suggested we go so he could meet Susie.

"I don't know," I said.

"He's your father, Susan. Just because he believes in UFOs, is that so terrible?"

Evan dialed my dad's number and handed me the phone. My dad sounded surprised by the call and thrilled at the suggestion.

"I'm speaking on Saturday afternoon, right before the Alien Parade," he said. "I'd love it if you'd come, hon. I can't wait to see Susie." His excitement made me feel even worse.

That Saturday we drove to McMinnville. The town was working the UFO theme for all its worth. The main street had closed to traffic and booths were selling all kinds of alien kitsch. A band in silver spacesuits and cowboy hats played bluegrass while people dressed in Star Trek uniforms or with their arms and faces painted green danced. More costumed revelers partied in the beer garden.

My dad's lecture was in the old theater on the main street. We found seats near the front so Susie could see, but on an aisle in case she started acting up. We'd bought her a pair of deely-boppers with glow-in-the-dark alien heads and she was having a wonderful time. So was Evan, who laughed every time he looked at her sitting between us like some happy little bug.

I couldn't see my dad anywhere, but a pony-tailed man in a t-shirt emblazoned with an anarchy symbol was aligning the slide projector. The theater gradually filled with a hundred or more people. The lights dimmed and the man adjusting the projector clambered onto the stage to introduce my dad, describing him as "one of the pre-eminent ufologists in the country."

Evan snorted. To modest applause my dad walked out to the podium. He was wearing a corduroy sport coat that lent him a professorial air. He had aged a lot since the wedding. Paunchier, balder. His glasses looked too big for his face.

"Look, Susie, that's your granddad," I said, emotion swelling my voice.

"Thank you, thank you. It's a pleasure to have this opportunity to present some of the exciting developments taking place in UFO research," he said with the same enthusiasm I remembered when he helped me with a math problem or explained the aurora borealis.

My dad began by describing the Trent case, which occurred near McMinnville in 1950 and was the reason they held the festival there. On the screen he showed grainy black and white photos the Trents had taken of a flying saucer hovering over their farm. He cited a 1968 investigation commissioned by the Air Force and the University of Colorado to determine if the photos had been doctored or staged and he quoted from the study's conclusion that they appeared to be untouched.

"These are some of the most extraordinary UFO photos ever taken," he told the audience.

"Now, as scientists, it's our job to sort through the evidence to determine what is truly unexplainable. As any ufologist worth his salt will tell you, what we are looking for is *proof*–physical evidence of alien interventions on earth. Most sightings tracked by UFOIN can be explained by natural or man-made causes. But nearly a third can't."

He flashed through a series of photos and drawings people had sent him of UFOs they'd seen. They all looked pretty lame. Blurry lights or sketches of saucers you'd see in a B-movie. One drawing looked just like a Philippe Stark fruit juicer I'd bought at Target. But my dad's presentation was the epitome of reasonable scientific description mixed with self-effacing humor.

After the slides he asked how many in the audience had ever seen a UFO, and a surprising number of people–almost half the room–raised their hands. My dad nodded excitedly. "Uh-huh, uh-huh. And how many of you believe you might have been abducted by aliens?"

Evan looked at me and raised his eyebrows, and the pudgy, round-shouldered man in front of me chortled, but a few people raised their hands.

"There you go, folks. It's nice to see you're not alone, isn't it? And this is just the tip of the iceberg.

"Today I want to share with you some truly important information. My colleagues and I believe we have found the best physical evidence yet of alien contact."

His voice had revved up the way it did whenever he told Mom and me about his classified work for the government, or later when he told my friends about seeing his first UFO. I started to get an uneasy feeling in my stomach.

"A year ago, a man in northern California contacted me to report that he'd been visited by aliens several nights in a row. Being a forensics investigator, he decided to capture them on film the next time they showed up, so he installed a motion-activated camera in the clock radio in his bedroom. And here's what he caught..."

He clicked the slide advance and a blurry image, like the x-ray of a raccoon, appeared on the screen. The room fell silent. "And this, ladies and gentlemen," he advanced to what looked like a dried-up cat turd on a piece of paper with a ruler beside it for scale, "this we believe to be a possible alien claw."

The man in front of me snickered and elbowed his friend.

"This evidence was discovered in the man's closet the day after he captured the aliens on film. We sent pieces of it out for analysis to authorities at the San Diego Zoo and to several DNA experts I happen to know in other countries.

"And guess what? No one was able to identify it!"

The next slide showed a letter from the San Diego Zoo with an underlined paragraph stating that the substance was not mammalian.

"We were about to publish this remarkable discovery when a colleague from Australia emailed to say he'd made a nearly perfect match. The DNA has a 95% match to a type of sea slug from the waters off New Zealand!

"Now, ladies and gentlemen, you tell me, how did a sea slug swim 14,000 miles to end up petrified in this man's closet?"

The man in front of me burst out laughing and covered his mouth with his hand.

"Were the aliens just playing a game, leaving behind a prank because the forensics specialist was on to them? Or is it a possible alien claw?"

He ended his presentation on that rhetorical note and opened the floor to questions.

Evan gave me an amused, quizzical look. I felt completely embarrassed; it was as if I were fourteen again and my dad was out on the patio staring up at the sky with his binoculars. The man in front of me was laughing and joking with his buddy. Then he raised his hand.

"Yes!" my dad said, pointing to him and stepping closer.

"Well, first of all, aren't we like a 99% match to most other mammals? So, what does your DNA match prove except that it's probably a slug? But just supposing it was a claw, how come they left it behind? I mean, if they're so smart?"

"Who knows," my dad said, shaking his head. "Look, for all we know, some alien rented a spaceship like you'd rent a car from Avis and said to his pal, 'Let's go to Earth for the weekend and scare some people.'"

The crowd laughed.

"Or, as many ufologists believe," and my dad's voice filled with ominous warning, "they could be tampering with our genetics."

The man in front of me raised his hand again.

"Yeah, I'd also like to know why they used flying saucers in the fifties and then after *Star Wars* they started using wedge-shaped spaceships. Did they make a technology change based on the movie?"

More laughter from the audience.

"I see we have a debunker in our midst," my dad said calmly, hitching up his pants as if girding for battle. "Is there any reason not to suppose we have been visited by aliens from more than one place, with more than one technology?"

"So maybe Hertz rents the wedge-shaped ones," jousted the man. My dad gamely laughed with the audience.

"Do we know what they look like?" asked another person.

"A good question, without an easy answer. It's likely there are all kinds. I like to use this analogy: Imagine if someone asked you to describe life on earth. Would you describe a giraffe or a whale? A cactus or a cockroach? We simply don't know the answer."

"We only have time for one more question," the emcee interrupted. "*Spaceballs* is showing in half an hour."

The man in front of me whispered something to his buddy then raised his hand again. I was beginning to get really angry. I couldn't understand why my dad continued to take his questions. Couldn't he see this jerk was making a fool of him?

"Yes," my dad said, pointing to the man again.

"Thanks. So, why isn't the government concerned about your findings?"

It was like flashing a lure in front of a hungry trout.

"That's an excellent question!" I could hear my dad's voice slip into hyperdrive. "The government *is* fully aware. They've been tracking UFOs longer than anyone. All of it classified, of course. As taxpayers, I can't understand why we let them keep up this campaign of disinformation. And it is a campaign, folks. I'm sure the military informs the President about the things they track. Ronald Reagan knew exactly what he was doing when he implemented the Star Wars program. And isn't it curious that he got Alzheimer's just as he left office! Could it be they didn't want him going public with what he knew?

"Another curious thing happened a few years later. Do any of you remember the time Bill Clinton fell down at Greg Normans' house in Florida and ended up having knee surgery? It was front-page news in all the papers. Well, coincidentally, at exactly the same time—March 13, 1997 at 2220 hours—there was a major UFO sighting over Phoenix. I received dozens of calls on the hotline. Now just picture it, the President is in an unfamiliar house when he's told of a major UFO sighting. Either he tripped as they were rushing him to safety, probably to an underground installation somewhere, or *maybe* it was all a manipulation to distract the press from reporting the sighting. Folks, if you ever get the chance to see President Clinton in shorts, look to see if there's a scar on his knee. And please, let me know!"

I was cringing. Not only had he taken the bait, he'd chomped down hard.

"By the way, I also have it from very high-up sources in the Air Force that they are fully aware of my organization's activities, and although they can't officially corroborate my suspicions, a lot of them tell me off the record to keep up the good work."

Shades of 1992 when my dad saw his UFO. The paranoia was oozing out for all to see. Even the man in front of me was reduced to silent laughter. My dad thanked the audience and after a brief applause the lights came up and the crowd started to leave.

I couldn't help it. I was so angry I reached over and tapped the man in front of me on the shoulder as he got up from his chair.

"I just wanted to say I thought you were really disrespectful and rude."

It took him a second to absorb what I'd said. "Hey, if you want to believe crap like that, that's your problem."

"Yeah? Well, next time keep your wise-ass comments to yourself."

"Aw, fuck off, lady."

"Hey, watch your language," Evan said as I snapped back, "Asshole!"

"Susan!" Evan said, but he rose to defend me.

Susie giggled so hard her deely-boppers were bouncing. "Mommy said 'asshole.'"

Evan was a lot bigger than the guy, who scoffed at me like I was some whacko and sauntered up the aisle talking loudly to his friend.

"What was that all about?" Evan asked.

I shook my head. "I'm sorry. Forget it. Let's go meet Dad."

I stood up. Evan picked up Susie and we worked our way down to the foot of the stage where my dad was talking to the emcee and someone from the audience who ponderously stroked a long gray Rumpelstiltskin beard.

My dad saw me from the corner of his eye and stopped what he was saying to come give me a hug. "I can't believe it's you, honey! I'm so glad you came. I saw you sitting behind that man who was asking all the questions. What did you think? Exciting stuff, isn't it?"

"Dad, this is Susie."

Susie was sitting on Evan's shoulders laughing happily.

"Susie, this is your granddad. Say hi."

"Hi," she said shyly.

"Gosh, hon, she's the spitting image of you."

A sad smile appeared on his face as he gazed up at Susie, and that did it. Maybe it was the rush of adrenaline from my encounter with the debunker, but I started to cry. For my crazy father and my lost teenage years and the family we'd once been. My dad didn't know what to make of my tears, so I hugged him again. He patted me on the back like he used to do and said it was all right. He'd missed me, too. That only made me cry more.

"Say, wouldn't Susie like to be in the parade?" he asked, as if to change the subject.

"I don't know, Dad." I wiped my eyes and looked at Evan.

"It's just down the main street. She'd be safe with me. We'll be riding in the back seat of a Model T."

"Parade!" Susie shouted, deely-boppers bouncing. Evan shrugged.

"Sure, Dad. She'd like that."

So that's how Susie came to ride in the UFO Parade down the main street of McMinnville. Evan and I stood along the route waiting as hawkers of flying saucer yo-yos and slime green cotton candy worked the crowd. We watched and cheered as the local high school band marched past, then a float depicting the Trent farmhouse with a flying saucer jutting from its broken roof. The obelisk from *2001: A Space Odyssey*—complete with waving chimpanzees—came next, followed by a truck with people dressed as Men in Black tossing candy to children. Then came the red Model T, and the crowd cheered again.

There was my dad, smiling and waving beneath a hand-painted sign, "Grand Marshal and World-Renowned Ufologist." And there was Susie, sitting beside him wearing her deely-boppers, laughing and having the time of her life like the little believer I used to be.

MENACE

"Mom, what's this?"

"What's what?"

John was in the dining room looking through a box of papers; his mother was in the kitchen making sandwiches. Despite the pass-through between the two rooms, they were shouting as if at opposite ends of the house.

"This box on the dining room table."

"Oh, that's my tax information. Leave it alone. I'm collecting it for Mr. Herman."

Mr. Herman, the octogenarian accountant. He continued to leaf through the papers. There were credit card receipts, property tax assessments, monthly investment statements, outdated proxies, and a manila envelope stuffed with cancelled checks.

"Mom, why are you including cancelled checks? What are you keeping them for anyway?"

"I've always kept them."

"But you don't need to. Your bank keeps copies. You can view them online."

"I hate computers. They make me feel stupid. I'm always losing things."

"You can't lose them. You're looking at their website."

"Well, somehow I do."

John Morrison had flown to Tucson the day before. He was in Los Angeles on business and decided to take a long weekend to go through his mother's finances and sift through the rising tide of clutter that seemed to envelop the townhouse. And, if he could do it without her noticing, he planned to fill the trunk of the rental car with the flotsam of his cleaning efforts and unload it at Goodwill on his way to the airport. Two full days before he headed back to Chicago.

His sister Ellen had warned him they needed to do something about her credit cards too. The last time she was there she discovered their mother had attached a miniature Visa card to her key chain. Her bank had sent it as a marketing ploy. It turned out to be a false alarm; their mother hadn't realized she needed to phone the bank to activate it. But that wasn't the point. It could have been, and it could have been left hanging there for the gas-station mechanic or the parking valet or the clerk in the grocery store to abuse. Their mother seemed oblivious to the risk.

Their father had died seven years earlier. Ever since, John and Ellen took turns visiting their mother and reported back on her state of affairs and state of mind. But it was hard to find the time. Ellen lived in Seattle and was dealing with young twins, and with his new promotion John had expanding responsibilities at the bank. Their best intentions of quarterly visits had fallen off to semi-annual stopovers. They encouraged their mother to spend a few weeks with each of them during the summer, but it wasn't quite the same. They needed to see how she was doing on her own turf. Yet somehow nearly a year had slipped by since his last visit.

"Mom, why do you have so many credit cards?"

"They keep sending them to me. I don't ask for them."

"Well, you don't need to use them. You should cut them up. Keep one or maybe two."

"Oh, no."

"Why not?"

No response. He could hear her taking plates from the cupboard and knew she'd heard him.

"You're always saying you feel overwhelmed by the bills," he persisted. "That way you wouldn't have to worry about all of these late charges."

"I don't like to see how much I'm spending."

He looked up from the box and his eyes focused on the silver-framed photograph of his father on the sideboard. He shook his head in disbelief. Had she always been so childish about financial matters or was this a sign of incipient dementia?

"Mom, what possible difference is there if you spend it all on one card or ten?"

"The department stores prefer me to use their card."

"Well, of course they do. But that doesn't mean you have to."

"I've had my Dillard's card for thirty years. I'm not giving it up now. Come and eat your sandwich."

He put the statements back in the box and went into the kitchen. His mother, still dressed in the cotton bathrobe she wore like a day coat, was making room on the round teak table, the same worn table that had been at the center of the kitchen in their house when he was a boy. Clutter was everywhere and John had to move a pile of clipped coupons from the chair in order to sit at the place his mother had set. To his left, through a window protected by wrought iron security bars, he could see the small cactus garden that served as her front yard and identical townhouses across the street. Beneath the window, cooking magazines and cookbooks were stacked and slanting along a bowed bookshelf. Opposite him, as if it were another guest at the table, a TV balanced on a small cabinet with more things piled around and on top of it. The table itself was littered with opened and unopened mail, catalogues, charity appeals for money and two remote controls. At the center, on a lazy Susan crowded with knick-knacks and jars of mustard, jam and marmalade, he recognized a repoussé silver bowl that had been his grandmother's. It was filled with Andes Mints and served as a paperweight for a stack of paper napkins.

When they moved their mother into the townhouse six years ago they kept as many of the things from the old house as they could. That hadn't helped with the clutter but at the time she was still grieving for their father and the familiar objects brought comfort. Now, whenever he visited, he experienced an uneasy feeling of familiarity in a place for which he had no memory, a kind of spatial dementia of his own.

On the wall above the telephone he noticed something new since his last visit—a clock shaped like a black cat, its black-and-white eyes and striped tail moving in counterpoint with each tick, stared down at him: quarter to twelve.

"Doctor Brady used to have a clock just like that in his office," he said. "I remember it was the only fun thing about visiting him."

"Did he?"

"Where'd you get it?"

"Target had them on sale. I thought it was cute. I was thinking of getting another one to send to the twins for their birthday. Would Vicky like one?"

"I don't think so, Mom. Vicky's sixteen going on twenty-six. She's into her cell phone."

"But wouldn't she think it's cute?"

"Only if a boy's attached. Thanks, Mom, but no." He looked up at the clock again. "Did Ellen hang it for you?"

"No. Sam, my handyman, did. That reminds me, he said he'd come by this morning to work on the irrigation. I don't know what's the matter with it but it's not going on properly and all of my flowers have died. I can't tell you how many times we've replaced the timer. The damn things keep breaking. I wonder where he is?"

She got up and took their plates to the sink.

"What would you like for dinner? I have some nice lamb chops in the freezer."

He was pretty sure she meant her second freezer, the one in the utility room that was so full you couldn't find anything in it. For all he knew the lamb was two years old.

"Let's go out tonight. I'm craving Mexican."

"John Junior! We had Mexican last night!"

"I know but I love it and it isn't the same in Chicago." Anything to avoid the lamb.

Later that afternoon they sat down together in the living room to watch *The Manchurian Candidate*; she'd bought the DVD at Sam's Club thinking he'd enjoy it. John didn't have the heart to tell her he'd already seen it.

A few minutes after it started he began to review her credit-card statements and was relieved to find no irregularities except the frequent late charges and interest payments.

"The original was much better," she said. "Wasn't that with Burt Lancaster?"

"I don't remember, Mom."

He was already feeling the exasperation that surfaced whenever he visited, the slide into his teenage defense of restlessness. He went to the kitchen to get a beer and was hunting for a bottle opener when the doorbell rang.

"I'll get it," he yelled.

He opened the door to a wiry man in his forties wearing yellow-tinted sunglasses and a green John Deere cap. A frayed flannel shirt cut off at the sleeves exposed lean but muscular arms tanned dark brown with a faded dragon tattoo breathing fire down the right forearm. A sheathed Buck knife hung from his belt.

The man seemed as startled as he was. "Oh, hi. Is Mrs. Morrison home?" A missing cuspid revealed as he smiled explained the slurred pronunciation of his mother's name. His face was thin and grizzled. Creases lined gaunt cheeks scarred by acne years before. He looked weathered, sandblasted. But more to the point, to John he had the unsavory look of a drug addict.

"And who are you?"

"I'm Sam. I'm here to fix the irrigation. Are you her son?"

The dots connected. The man who'd hung the clock. The handyman. "Ah! Yes, sorry. I'm John Morrison."

He extended his hand, feeling slightly embarrassed by his initial reaction.

Sam's hand felt leathery and calloused, as hard as a piece of wood. Behind the sunglasses John saw a shiftiness he still didn't like.

"Tell your mom I'm missing some parts and need to go to the Home Depot. Does she want to give me cash or should I add it to the bill?"

"How much are we talking about?"

"Maybe twenty bucks."

"Oh. Then add it to the bill."

"I probably won't get it finished today," Sam said.

"I'll let her know."

Sam turned and cut through the carport to his truck. John noticed his hair was gathered in a wispy ponytail that fell below the collar of his shirt. He watched as Sam climbed up into the cab of a red Ford pickup with a missing tailgate and a truck-bed scraped raw. The truck rumbled as he started it—obviously missing part of a muffler too.

"Who was that, honey?" his mother asked as he came back into the living room.

"Sam."

"Has he fixed the irrigation?"

"No, he said he needs to get some parts. Where'd you find him anyway?"

"Sam?"

"Yes."

"Through Maria."

"Your cleaning lady?"

"Uh-huh."

"Well, what do you know about him?"

"He's been very helpful. He's fixed all kinds of things for me."

John glanced around the room acknowledging there was much bordering on disrepair. He felt bad he wasn't better at fixing things himself. But he was a banker, not a handyman.

"Besides, he's had a tough life. He's an alcoholic, you know."

"How do you know that?"

"Don't be silly. He told me."

"Mom, you need to be careful who you let in your house."

"He's a friend of Maria's."

"That's fine. But you don't know anything about him, do you?"

"I know enough. He needs the work. He moved here from El Paso and has been trying to start over. He goes to AA. Be a Christian for heaven's sake!"

"Start over! From what? Prison?"

His mother smirked. "When did you become so condescending?"

"Do you give him cash?"

"Well, I have to pay him."

"He just asked for some cash to buy things."

"Well, sometimes we do it that way. He doesn't have much himself. Stop being such a control freak, John."

She picked up a magazine with an annoyed flourish even though the movie was still on. He had taken his point as far as he dared. In her mind there was a fine line between his watching out for her and outright meddling. Any further and she would lay recriminations at his feet: How he wasn't there often enough to know better. How she was alone and had to make decisions.

But, thinking again about the encounter with Sam, he couldn't quite stop himself.

"How'd he know I was your son?"

She didn't even look up from her magazine. "I *told* him you were coming. Any more questions?"

He sipped his beer. After fifty years he knew when he'd tested the limit.

The next day he attacked the clutter. The bedroom where he was sleeping reeked of mothballs and was filled with junk: in the closet, under the bed, on the bookshelves, even in the dresser drawers. Cheap gifts mostly she had bought thinking she'd give them to someone someday. Not that she had anyone in mind specifically. When he arrived and was putting his bag in the guest room his mother had picked up a dusty box of fruit slices lying on the dresser and offered them to him.

"You used to love these," she said.

"When I was ten, Mom. No thanks."

He began in the closet. Two pink ceramic piggy banks from the Dollar Store. A set of "special offer" Mirro pots and pans. Commemorative Raggedy Ann and Andy dolls. A dozen large-format, full-color "Cuisines of the World" cookbooks from Barnes & Noble. A jar of candied ginger from Trader Joe's. A 16-piece set of white "Elements" china from Target.

Correction: two sets, the second still in a bag with the receipt, bought the year before—$34.99.

"Mom, what were you planning to do with this stuff?"

"I thought you kids might like it."

"I don't want these," he said, holding up a croquet set made in Pakistan.

"Well, maybe Ellen does."

"Mom, it'll cost more to ship than it's worth."

"Fine, then I'll give it to Maria."

"Well, that would be better, but I doubt Maria wants it."

"Then I'll give it to the church. They're having a rummage sale in a few weeks. They can always use things."

"Fine."

He was barely able to move amid the piles he had pulled out.

"You're making a big mess, John! I had Maria put that all neatly away before you got here."

He started to take things out to his car.

"Now what are you doing?"

"I'm taking it up to the church."

"Not the china! That's perfectly good. Somebody can use that."

"Fine, Mom. I'll leave one set."

His mother retreated to her bedroom where she was pretending to straighten things up. He knew she had clothes and shoes and jewelry scattered around the room. But he would let Ellen deal with those more personal things.

"Would you like to go with me?" he offered as he opened the front door, keys in hand.

"Where?"

"Really, Mom? To the church."

"No. Just leave it in the box in the vestibule and be sure to let the office know."

"Okay. I'll be back in a while."

The church was a mile further up the road in the Santa Catalina foothills. It was April and the heat was already building but the ocotillos had leafed out from a recent rain. As he drove into the church parking lot he could see far up Pima Canyon. The pink mountains dappled with blue-gray shadows from a few clouds made him homesick even though he hadn't lived in Tucson for thirty years.

He was in a happier mood driving back, the trunk emptied of its load. He hoped his mother would be feeling better too. He turned onto his mom's street and saw Sam's big red truck in the carport occupying his space beside his mom's car. He pulled to the curb in front of her house. As he got out of the car Sam came around the corner of the townhouse. He was wearing the same green cap and yellow-tinted sunglasses but a different shirt, this one faded denim also cut off at the sleeves, and he was holding a roll of black plastic tubing.

"Sorry. I thought you'd gone already."

"Nope, still here."

"Want me to move it?"

"No, that's okay."

Sam nodded and went back around the corner of the house. John went inside. His mother was in the living room reading. The TV was also on, muted, tuned to CNN.

"I see your handyman's back."

"Yes, he came after you left."

The sliding glass door to her back patio was open halfway. "It was stuffy in here," she explained when he asked why. Through the door they could see Sam near the thin patch of flowerbed. He was kneeling beside a drip line, making adjustments.

"Does he just come and go as he pleases?" he whispered. "How do you know how much to pay him?"

"Who, Sam?" Clearly she was not about to modulate her voice to appease him. "Honestly, John. I pay him ten dollars an hour. I know how much time he spends here."

He watched Sam work. He disliked this stranger having complete access to his mother's house. He was thinking about all of the things his mother left around and the exploding number of identity theft cases they dealt with at the bank.

"Don't your neighbors have a handyman?"

"Sure. They use Sam. Got him from me."

He left it at that. He went to his room and called home to see how things were going. From the window he kept his eye on Sam while he talked to his daughter then to his wife. Sam kept getting up and disappearing around the side of the house to turn the system on or off. He'd make adjustments and disappear again. He seemed to know what he was doing. He seemed to be working steadily. Maybe his mother was right after all.

He rejoined her in the living room. A short while later Sam knocked on the open door. John stood up and approached so he wouldn't come inside.

"Well, I think it's all fixed."

"Oh, thank you, Sam," his mother said from the couch. "What was it?"

"Far as I can tell it was them feeder lines going into the main." He directed the explanation at John. "There's these little emitters attached at the main line that get corroded from the hard water or sometimes they get blocked by sand. Anyway, most of 'em needed replacing."

John nodded.

"So it wasn't the timer then?" his mother asked.

"Nope. Far as I can tell, the timer's all right. Everything seems to be working fine now."

"Well, thank goodness. You must be hot, Sam. Would you like something to drink? And what do I owe you?"

"No thanks, ma'am. It'll be thirty dollars for this one. Plus parts." He looked at John. "Fifteen-sixty-three. You want the receipt?"

"Yes," he said at the same time his mother said no.

He got out his wallet, counted fifty dollars and handed them to Sam.

"Remind me to write you a check before you go, honey," his mother said.

Sam made a motion to dig for change.

"That's fine. Keep it," he said.

"Oh, Sam!" His mother got up suddenly from the couch. "Hang on." She hurried into the dining room and came back with the set of china John had pulled from the closet. "Would you be able to use this? My son was going to give it away but I thought you might like it."

"What is it, Mrs. Morrison?" Sam asked. The eyes behind the yellow-tinted sunglasses shifted from his mother to John and back again.

"It's bone china. Just a set of four four-piece place settings but I thought it looked very nice."

Sam seemed puzzled, uncertain how to respond. "Well, sure, I guess." He turned the box sideways to look at the label then opened the lid as if to verify its contents. "Thanks very much." He looked at John. "This okay?"

"Please," he said.

"Thanks much," Sam said again. "Anything else you need me for, Mrs. Morrison?"

"Not right now, Sam. My toilet's been running a little but let's wait until my son's gone to fix it. I'll call you next week."

"Sure, no problem." Then, eyes shifting back to John: "Don't forget your car's on the street."

"Thanks," John said. He slid the door shut and locked it.

His mother was sitting on the couch again, a smirk on her face.

"So there."

He wasn't sure if she was feeling vindicated about Sam or the set of china.

"What?"

"I told you someone would be happy to have it."

That evening she cooked the lamb chops she had offered him the night before. They washed the dishes together and watched part of *Finding Neverland*, but by nine o'clock she said she was exhausted and, apologizing, went to bed. John packed and then sat in the living room sipping a beer. He could hear his mother's light snores and found himself listening for each exhalation. He poured the last third of the beer into the kitchen sink and went to bed.

The next morning, despite telling her he'd eat something at the airport, she got up early to make him breakfast. It was Sunday; she was going to church anyway, she said. At the front door they hugged. He urged her to visit them in July while Vicky was out of school and promised to bring the family the next time he came to Tucson. She became teary as he left.

Thanks to his frequent flyer status he boarded the plane in the first grouping. Sitting by the window, he watched people trundle their carry-ons down the narrow aisle, hoist their bags to the overhead compartments, stuff items in seat pockets and squeeze themselves into seats. The jostling in the crowded space made him think of his mother. He always felt bad when he left, knowing he'd spent too little time with her. The short cycling of emotions was hard on her. First, the anticipation of his arrival, then the initial excitement caused by his presence that somehow always twisted into recriminations, and then the sadness of his departure. It was hard on him too. He never knew if he would see her again. He also worried the day was approaching when she would need more care. She seemed unconcerned. Was that blithe denial of what could go wrong or elderly stubbornness? He felt his responsibility and his worry like a heavy weight.

As the plane taxied onto the runway, he managed to push these concerns from his mind and think about home. A moment later the plane took off. It climbed steeply then banked in a sharp turn. John felt the press of gravity against his body and found himself looking almost straight down at the empty desert below. He glimpsed a red truck speeding along a remote dirt road, churning up a cloud of dust. Panic sucked the breath from him. He felt dizzy and claustrophobic, as if he were bound and gagged and tumbling through the air. He shut his eyes only to see Sam, or a man more insidious, more dangerous, roll down the truck's window, grab the box rattling on the seat beside him and hurl it into an arroyo. He saw the box burst and the china explode in bright jagged shards. And on the man's face he saw pleasure in the wanton destruction, a sneering contempt for his mother's powerless protector, and menace in his eyes.

THE
LAST
RUN

Charles Dawson—to use the name he went by—entered the dining room of the pensión just as the other guests were seating themselves.

"Señor Dávila, I'm expecting an important call tonight. Will you let Marta know? I'll be up in my room."

"Good evening, Mr. Dawson. Of course! But won't you join us for supper?"

As Señor Dávila spoke Marta came through the swinging door from the kitchen carrying a steaming platter of enchiladas suizas and a bowl of frijoles negros. Charles Dawson had been drinking with Jaime in the Zona Rosa. The food looked inviting.

"Why not!"

He surveyed the other guests as he removed his Panama hat and placed it on the antique sideboard. He chose the chair beside an attractive woman with short blond hair. "Buenas noches," he said, nodding to the group.

There was only one telephone in the Casa Dávila. It was on the wall of the veranda facing the courtyard garden. Whenever it rang the pensión's guests could hear the housekeeper or the cook or Señor Dávila himself answer it in Spanish or English depending on the person on the other end.

Charles Dawson liked this arrangement—the intermediary aspect of it. It was better than having a phone in his room even though it meant conversations had to be carefully phrased. After all, if he could hear every word from his room, so could everyone else in the other rooms surrounding the courtyard.

He stayed at the Casa Dávila whenever he came to Mexico City. He preferred the low-keyed pensión to a hotel despite the unavoidable intimacy among the guests. Meals, for instance, were shared in the wood-paneled dining room that opened through French doors onto the veranda. At breakfast and dinner Señor Dávila often presided at the table, engaging in conversation and striving to make his guests feel welcome.

Señor Dávila was a stocky, barrel-chested man in his early sixties with a smooth round face and closely cropped silver hair encircling a bald spot on the crown of his head. He dressed with casual flair, his clothes always looking immaculate, and he seemed to have a fondness for pastel colors. He exuded both the energy of an entrepreneur and the nonchalance of inherited wealth. The Casa, he explained, had been in his family for four generations. Running it as a pensión was something he did as much for pleasure as for profit. Since his family now spent most of its time at a second home in Cuernavaca, the elegant old mansion would otherwise be empty and too expensive to maintain.

At the table, Señor Dávila had a talent for drawing out even the hardest-shelled guests. That too appealed to Charles Dawson, who in his own way saw himself as a student of humanity. He enjoyed disclosing a few personal tidbits, even if they were made up, to a group of strangers he would never see again.

This evening only four other guests were at the table. A dentist and his wife from Denver were staying two nights to see the Diego Rivera murals before flying to Puerto Vallarta for a week at the Camino Reál. A Guatemalan civil engineer who lived in Brooklyn was going home to visit his sick father. And the attractive blond seated next to him, a nurse from Seattle, was on her way to the Yucatán. She had paid good money to some non-profit outfit to spend her vacation working at an archaeological site near Tulúm.

It amused Charles Dawson almost as much as it pleased Señor Dávila that these details had been volunteered at the slightest inquiry. But now, in an awkward silence punctuated by the clinking of silverware, he saw that the others were waiting for him to say something, as if this were an AA meeting and it was his turn to come clean.

"When I arrived at the airport yesterday–" He turned to direct his words to the nurse, having noticed the top buttons of her blouse were undone, revealing a lacey edge of brassiere and just a shadow of cleavage.

"Yes, Mr. Dawson?" Señor Dávila's eyes actually seemed to sparkle with encouragement.

"Did you know you can get a driver's license there for only five thousand pesos?" He watched for a reaction. "An official license right at the airport. You don't even have to show them an ID or take a test. Can you believe it?"

"Is that so?" said Señor Dávila.

"Sure. Look." He reached into the inside pocket of his cream-colored linen suit and took out his wallet. He unfolded the document. Seeing it again, he smiled. The black-and-white photo was badly taken and overdeveloped, washed out from too much flash like a mug shot. His eyes were half shut; his lips set in a thin line. His face looked featureless–ashen skin, colorless blond hair, a receding hairline augmented by the white glare.

He handed it to the nurse.

"Oh, this is just one of those international driver's licenses," she said. "It's not like it's good for anything."

"I could have put any name I wanted on it."

"I don't understand. Why would you want to do that?"

Amused by her puzzled expression, he smiled. "I'm just saying I could have."

The nurse passed the license to Señor Dávila at the head of the table.

"They required an address in Mexico," Charles Dawson said, "so I used Casa Dávila. I hope you don't mind."

Señor Dávila was studying the license and seemed at a momentary loss for words. "If this is where you feel at home, Mr. Dawson, then I am honored." He offered the license to the civil engineer and it went around the table until it came back to Charles Dawson.

The telephone rang and Marta ran from the kitchen to the veranda to answer it.

"Bueno?"

"Where're you from, Charlie?" asked the dentist.

"One moment please," Marta said in her deliberate English. She came into the dining room and fetched Señor Dávila. "Someone wants to reserve a room," she said in Spanish.

"Excuse me," Señor Dávila said, leaving the table. Charles Dawson noticed the dentist was still staring, waiting for an answer.

"Oh–I travel around a lot. Phoenix mainly."

"Huh, I thought I detected a Missouri accent."

"Nope. I spent some time in Arkansas," he said, pleased with his phrasing. It wasn't a lie.

"Little Rock? My brother lives there."

"No."

Charles Dawson had had enough fun and the woman next to him didn't show any interest. He swallowed the last of his coffee and excused himself from the table. "Buen provecho," he said to the others with a smile and a tip of the Panama hat. It was a phrase he had picked up from Señor Dávila. Somehow it gave him a pleasant sense of belonging in Mexico, of extending hospitality rather than accepting it. He went upstairs to wait for his call.

He discovered the Casa Dávila on his first trip to Mexico. He had crossed the border at Nogales and bought a train ticket to Mexico City, figuring it was the best place to go to conduct his business. At the train station in Guadalajara he ran into a friendly German kid with a bulging backpack who had stayed at the pensión the week before. "Cash only but very reasonable. Right in the center," the kid said, generously tearing the page out of his *Rough Guide* and handing it to him.

It was after midnight when he rang the bell at the locked gate across the driveway. A high stone wall protected the grounds of the house from the street; he could see the jagged outline of broken bottles set in mortar at the top to deter thieves. After a few minutes a light turned on and the housekeeper, whose name he later learned was Marta, came down the path shaking her head vigorously and saying something in a rapid Spanish. He couldn't understand except in the context of her motions.

"But I telephoned from Guadalajara," he lied, not realizing how transparent the lie would be, given the single telephone in the Casa. "And the taxi's gone." He pointed to the suitcase behind him on the sidewalk.

He still couldn't fully understand what she was saying, but finally she produced a large brass key ring from the folds of a heavy cotton skirt and opened the gate.

"Thank you, señora. I'm very grateful," he said in mangled Spanish.

He followed the squat middle-aged woman with the long black braid as she walked briskly up the drive. Walking past the main entrance of the house, she continued down a path to an arched opening in the wall that led into a large inner courtyard smelling of orange blossoms and damp earth. Water splashed softly in a fountain nearby. On the steps of a tiled veranda she turned and told him to leave his suitcase there. Then she led him inside the main house. She switched on a light and he followed her down a hallway lined with antique photographs into what looked like a living room with exposed beams spanning the breadth of a high ceiling. The spacious room was decorated with heavy pieces of mahogany furniture upholstered in dark brown leather. At a large claw-foot desk Marta opened a tattered register and handed him a pen. He wrote "Charles Dawson" in the space provided and gave an address in Tucson. Marta's tone was now deferential. She thanked him for his patience and handed him a key. She led him out to the veranda again, across the courtyard, and up a flight of outside stairs to a room on the second floor in another wing of the house.

"Mr. Dawson, welcome to Casa Dávila," Señor Dávila greeted him the next morning. He was wearing a pale blue guayabera with neatly pressed khaki slacks and tasseled Italian loafers. He crossed the dining room to shake Charles Dawson's hand. "I'm sorry for any inconvenience last night. We seem to have misplaced your reservation, which I assure you is not typical at Casa Dávila. I'm so glad we had a room available. The room is satisfactory?"

"Thank you. Yes."

It was nearly ten and the other guests had already come and gone. The remains of breakfast were being cleared. With an imperious tone Señor Dávila ordered the cook to prepare whatever Mr. Dawson wanted.

"This is your first time in Mexico City, Mr. Dawson?"

"Yes."

"Business or pleasure?"

He would later discover these were the same questions Señor Dávila asked each of his guests with the same friendly curiosity. But at the time he answered cautiously.

"Both," he said, slicing a piece of ripe cantaloupe with his spoon.

"Yes? Very good, very good! Well, I hope you will have the opportunity to enjoy some of the wonderful things our city has to offer—Chapúltepec Park, Bellas Artes, the anthropology museum, or the pyramids perhaps."

But he only stayed a few days that first trip. He met Sergio, who was a bouncer at a nightclub in the Zona Rosa, and Sergio introduced him to Jaime. They quickly worked out a small cash transaction, just a trial for both parties.

The next time he drove down from McAllen in a stolen BMW with a trunk full of computer hardware. It had been Jaime's idea: "Man, you can name your price for that shit down here. The car, too, cabrón!"

On the way down he decided to check out San Miguel de Allende where he'd heard there were lots of Americans taking art and Spanish classes. It was there, in a restaurant-bar off the zócalo, that he met Linda—a pretty, redheaded teacher from Chicago.

"You remind me of William Hurt in one of my all-time-favorite movies," she said, boldly removing the straw fedora from his head.

"Which one? *The Big Chill?*"

"No, silly. *Body Heat.*"

He ended up spending a month in San Miguel, improving his Spanish and moving in with her. Together they drove down to Mexico City so he could conclude his business. This time he phoned the Casa in advance.

Things went pretty well between them until the day she found out about her passport. He had sold it to Jaime without telling her. He didn't think she'd react the way she did. "How could you do that to me?" she asked. He could think of lots of reasons: because it was there, because it was easy, because he could. Instead he said, "What's the big deal. You can get a replacement at the embassy. Just tell them you lost it. I'll pay for it."

"You don't even know what it is to be honest, do you?" she said, her voice filled with disappointment.

The next day, while he was out with Jaime selling the car, she left. "I can't be with a man I can't trust," she wrote in the note he found in the room. "I hoped you were more than a small-time con man."

It was ironic really. She never would have known enough to say that if he hadn't confided he'd done some time for hanging paper. "What's that?" she asked naively. "Forging checks," he had to explain.

Still, her words burned. That was when he told Jaime he was tired of this nickel-and-dime shit. He wanted to be introduced to his sources.

Charles Dawson couldn't sleep. He waited all evening for the phone call but it never came. Was something going wrong with the deal? What had Jaime said? "These guys are the real deal, cabrón. Be straight with them or they will bury you in a field."

Around six in the morning he heard Marta and the cook stirring in the kitchen and decided to get up. He went downstairs before breakfast to settle his bill, using the crisp new twenties Señor Dávila appreciated so much.

"The señor has gone to Cuernavaca for the weekend," Marta explained as she put the money inside the desk drawer and locked it with one of her many keys. "He will be sad not to say good-bye," she said politely.

Charles Dawson nodded.

"Marta, I'm still expecting a phone call. Muy importante."

"Sí, señor."

He went upstairs to pack and opened the window to listen for the phone. In the courtyard Marta's little girl was playing on the grass, twirling in circles with her arms outstretched. Her long black hair radiated from her head as she incanted some gibberish in a squeaky sing-song voice. He guessed she was five or six. She wore a white embroidered cotton dress and her legs looked like little brown sticks.

The telephone rang and he listened carefully as Marta answered.

"Bueno?"

For a moment all he could hear was the little girl singing off-key.

"Bueno?" Marta said again, shushing her daughter.

"El señor no está," she repeated. "No here," she said slowly.

Whoever it was finally understood. Marta hung up and went back into the kitchen. The little girl began to sing again, jumping a make-believe hopscotch on the stepping-stones that cut across the lawn.

He continued to pack. He put his razor and shaving cream into a plastic bag and carefully placed it in the side pocket of the suitcase. He noticed his heart was thumping, set off by the ringing of the telephone. He pulled a leather holster from the bottom of the suitcase and strapped it around his shoulder. Then he took the compact Smith and Wesson from a nylon camera case and loaded the magazine. He slipped the gun into the holster and adjusted the fit. He put on the jacket of his suit and buttoned the lapels, making sure the gun didn't show.

After he closed and latched the suitcase he sat down on the bed and opened his briefcase. He counted the envelopes again and just to be sure counted the bills in each envelope. He closed the briefcase and turned the combination to lock it. He adjusted the Panama hat on his head and looked in the mirror. The same pale face on the driver's license stared back at him. He recalled what Jaime had said, partly in jest, the first time they met: "All you pinche gringos look alike, like you've never seen the sun before. You should wear something to help us tell you apart." That was when he bought the bleached hat and the linen suit. Like a ghost.

Now he looked around the spare little room to ensure nothing was forgotten. He picked up his suitcase in one hand and his briefcase in the other and descended the stairs to the courtyard to wait for the call.

He rested the bag on the veranda and sat down with his briefcase on a stone bench in the garden. The morning sun was already hot, a ghostly white disk glowing through the haze above the city. He felt a slight tingle of perspiration building under his arms but he kept his suit jacket buttoned. He stretched his legs.

Marta's little girl was sitting on the steps of the veranda singing vaguely and leafing through a children's book. Marta and the cook were in the kitchen. Amid their chatter came the dull banging of pots and the intermittent spray of water. From time to time Marta called to her daughter through the kitchen window to ensure she was nearby. "Sí, mamá, sí," the girl answered absently.

The blond nurse came down the stairs from her room, fanny pack and tennis shoes on, guidebook in hand.

"Hola," the little girl said shyly as the nurse went up the steps of the veranda.

"Hola," the nurse repeated, laughing.

"Pita, don't bother the guests," her mother shouted through the kitchen window.

"I'm not," the girl said impatiently.

The nurse went into the dining room and came out with an orange. Without even glancing his way she passed by Charles

Dawson toward the front entrance. He heard the gate clink shut. Bitch, he thought.

"Hola," the girl said, her voice as soft as a bird's chirp. She waved at him from the veranda. When he ignored her, she made a face at him.

He removed his hat. The sunlight fell pleasantly on his face, warming the top of his head. He could hear the fanning wings of a hummingbird in the purple bougainvillea on the wall behind him. The fragrance of citrus from one of the trees nearby filled his nose. He tried to settle his nerves by closing his eyes and breathing in the scent, but he was unable to stop thinking about his deal. On one hand he was afraid it was called off; on the other he was anxious it was happening.

If the phone rings, that's it. This is the last fucking time, he said to himself. He was too old for this. He would buy some land back in Missouri and settle down. He imagined the house he'd build and a woman like Linda he'd share it with.

"Léeme un cuento."

He started from his reverie. The girl had crept up beside him and was holding a book up to him. Large brown eyes stared at him from a waif-like face. She giggled at his confusion.

"Read me a story," she repeated, this time with cajoling insistence. On her breath he could smell the corn tortillas she'd eaten for breakfast. No longer shy, she leaned against his leg and, laughing again, crouched down to look up at him.

"Why don't you read it to yourself," he said in his flat American Spanish, feeling uncomfortable with her closeness.

"Because – I – want – you – to," she said, tapping his leg with each word. "Please!"

He took the worn, cardboard covered book she held out to him. It looked faintly familiar. On the cover was a drawing of a green room with a window, a fireplace and, above the mantel, a picture of a cow jumping over the moon. *Buenas noches, Luna.*

"In the great green room," began Charles Dawson, "there was a telephone and a red balloon and a picture of–" The girl nibbled on a strand of her hair and leaned against him until he was obliged to lift her onto his lap. He turned the page and she laughed, not so much at the story, he suspected, as at having conned him into reading it to her, "–the cow jumping over the moon."

The telephone clanged and Marta came rushing out of the kitchen again, wiping her hands on her skirt. "Lupita!" she scolded as she lifted the receiver. The girl leapt off Charles Dawson's lap.

"Yes, yes. One moment, please."

Marta waved to him.

"Señor Dawson, it's for you."

He felt his heart pound as he pressed the receiver to his ear.

"Hello? Yes... Yes, I have it. Right, five minutes... Right."

He put the phone down and took a deep breath. The little girl was peeking at him from the doorway of the kitchen.

"Lupita!" her mother warned. The girl gave him a conspiratorial smile but he was too absorbed in his plans now to pay any attention. He felt for his gun in the holster and lifted the suitcase from the step. With his other hand he put the Panama hat on his head and picked up the briefcase.

"Adios," he said toward the kitchen.

Marta came to the doorway. "Goodbye, señor. Have a safe journey."

In her squeaky voice the girl parroted her mother's words, Que le vaya bién, and giggled.

Charles Dawson nudged open the heavy wrought-iron gate with his suitcase. The gate swung shut behind him, clanking into its latch. He rested the suitcase on the sidewalk and let his eyes adjust to the white glare of the street. A beggar woman huddled in the shadow of the wall. At the sight of him she opened her hand and whispered an entreaty. He turned and looked the other way. A garbage truck rumbled past in a cloud of dirty exhaust. Four men, looking like bandits with bandanas covering their mouths, clung to its sides.

It had once been an elegant residential street but was now fully absorbed by the city. Parked cars lined both sides of the street from one end of the block to the other. According to Señor Dávila, many of the houses dated from the reign of Emperor Maximilian. He liked to show his guests a photograph from the days of Porfirio Díaz when the street was cobblestone and lined with shade trees. The trees were long gone. Several embassies had acquired the larger homes, discreetly identified by flags fluttering from poles above imposing walls. But others had been replaced by apartment buildings. Across the street, one of the distinguished old houses, damaged in the big earthquake several years earlier, had been torn down, creating a rent in the wall of affluence. Patchwork hovels of wood scrap and corrugated sheet metal had been erected in the breach, as if neither rich nor poor were bothered by the contrast but rather drew comfort from each other's proximity. It was what Charles Dawson loved about Mexico—everything jumbled together, anything possible.

A black Chevy Camaro with tinted windows turned the corner and veered toward him. The loud, muscular engine revved as the car lurched to a stop in the middle of the street. A young man wearing a leather jacket and chrome-colored sunglasses stepped out on the passenger side and nodded to him. Charles Dawson picked up his suitcase, but the man grabbed it from him, shoved it into the trunk and indicated for him to get in the car. Charles Dawson smiled uneasily—they seemed awfully young—and patted his breast pocket as if checking for his wallet. Taking a deep breath, briefcase in hand, he lifted the front seat and climbed into the back. The young man with the chrome sunglasses dropped the seat into place and hopped in. He said something to the driver that made both men laugh. As the car pulled away Charles Dawson—to use the name he went by—glanced back to see the little girl's thin face peering between the iron bars of the gate. She was giggling as she waved goodbye.

SABOTAGE

I'm not sure I should be telling this. Certainly Julio wouldn't, but then he's dead. What I mean is, even if he weren't dead, he couldn't be trusted to tell it. Artists are dishonest creatures really. They foist their version of reality upon us while making it all up. Writers, painters, actors, auteurs–they're all the same.

This happened in Barcelona in 1974. I was taking a year off after college to travel around Europe and was staying in a small two-star hotel on the Ramblas, the name of which I have long since forgotten. Worn and nondescript, it was located in a long block of shops and doorways with nothing more than the word "Hotel" stenciled in white letters on a blue awning above the door. Amid the colorful distractions of the Ramblas, the hotel was easily overlooked. I often walked right past it until I devised a foolproof method for keeping track of its location. If I was walking up the Ramblas, I'd pass the bird sellers, turn right before the flower stalls, and there the hotel would be, directly across the boulevard. (Of course, coming down the Ramblas, I'd pass the flower stalls and turn left before the bird sellers.)

Barcelona back then was more a city of possibilities than the trendy, affluent cosmopolis it has become. General Franco's face still appeared on television each night as the networks signed off but, sensing the old man's days were numbered, the Catalans were beginning to reclaim their cultural independence. A bustling energy was building. Proud cab drivers spoke of their city's "destiny." And yet, a provincial quality lingered, a feeling of life lived at a more leisurely pace. Laundry hung from balconies in the narrow streets of La Ribera. Prostitutes and transvestites leaned in the doorways of seedy Gothic Quarter bars. And on the wide avenues of L'Eixample small shops displayed odd assortments of olive oil, cheese, candied fruit, stationery, and handmade wooden toys.

That's why it was big news when Michelangelo Antonioni, the Italian director, arrived to shoot scenes for his next movie, *The Passenger*. An article in *La Vanguardia* reported that Jack Nicholson and Maria Schneider had the leading roles. Antonioni, the article continued, was one of Europe's great avant-garde directors, known for his technical mastery, strict aesthetics, spare landscapes, and characters whose alienation matched the physical worlds they inhabit. I'd seen *Blow-up* when it came out (which I'd just discovered was based on a short story by Julio Cortázar, whose books I was devouring after coming across a copy of *End of the Game* in a used bookstore), and another in black and white called *L'Avventura*. I pretty much agreed with the newspaper's assessment.

To my surprise, the morning after I read this article, I was going to leave my hotel to go to the corner café with my newly acquired copy of Cortázar's *A Manual for Manuel*, when a black-capped policeman in the lobby blocked my way. A film crew, he informed me, was about to shoot a scene in front of the hotel.

Through the dingy red-curtained window I saw the street was cordoned off and a small crowd had gathered on the sidewalk. The clerk at the front desk apologized and assured me the delay would only be a few minutes. He ignored the ringing phone to join the policeman and me as we watched a small army of technicians run cables for lights and rearrange café tables and chairs on the Rambla, all directed by an intense, middle-aged man with dark, wavy hair in a blue-and-white-striped rugby shirt.

"Look! That's Señor Antonioni," the clerk said.

The policeman nodded. "Yes, the maestro himself."

Antonioni was talking to Jack Nicholson, who was dressed like an American tourist in a light blue shirt and dark blue slacks. The director had one hand on his leading man's shoulder and was explaining something—perhaps the movement of the camera or an emotion he wanted to convey. Nicholson nodded. There was a sudden commotion as extras, cameramen, soundmen and gaffers scurried to their places. Then Nicholson approached the entrance of our hotel and smiled at the three of us on the other side of the revolving door. He pushed the door around full circle and, on cue, stepped out as if leaving the hotel to cross the street to the Rambla. Next to a bird seller's stall he halted as if he'd seen a ghost. He slipped around the corner of the stall, dashed back across the street, sidestepping through oncoming traffic, and ducked into a shoeshine shop.

That was the take. Antonioni, who had been peering into a viewer beside the cameraman, looked up and nodded, which triggered a new commotion as the crew started to dismantle equipment. The police opened the barricades, and the crowd began to disperse. The long-faced policeman in our lobby turned to me and said, "OK." I went outside and navigated through the crowd to the café on the corner.

After the commotion died down, I was sitting at a table by the window, reading my book, drinking a *café con leche* and nibbling on an *ensaimada*, when a good-looking man in his late fifties or early sixties wearing a gray tweed sport coat over a black turtleneck sweater entered the café and walked up to the counter. I did a double take, looking at the photo on the back of my book and then at the man again. He looked just like Julio Cortázar.

Just then a large woman in a bright pink raincoat leading a child by the hand stepped into my line of sight. I leaned back to get a better look. There was definitely a Gallic air about the man. He stood proudly erect and, when he turned sideways to glare at the whining child, I noted his dark sideburns and strong jawline. He took a long drag on his cigarette and turned away.

But could it really be Julio Cortázar? From my reading I knew he lived in Paris, not Barcelona.

I tried to get a better look but the man suddenly tossed his cigarette to the floor, crushed it under his shoe and left the café without ordering. I jumped up and hastened to follow. If it was Cortázar, I'd ask him to autograph my book.

By the time I got outside he was already turning the corner, walking rapidly up Calle de la Boqueria. I quickened my pace and saw him cut left toward the Plaza del Pi. I still wasn't certain it was Cortázar. The man turned into the entrance of a hotel framed by two ornamental trees in stone planters. I followed him inside.

It was a much nicer hotel than mine, with plush green carpeting and crystal chandeliers lighting a muted, wood-paneled lobby. As my eyes adjusted to the dim light I peered around, but he was nowhere to be found. I asked the doorman if he had seen the man in the gray sport coat. He smirked and hunched his shoulders. At the rear of the lobby three marble steps and a wide landing led to the elevator and the frosted-glass door to the bar. The light above the elevator indicated it was going up. I went over to the front desk and asked the pretty receptionist if Julio Cortázar was staying there.

"I'm sorry, sir," she said, shaking a head of lustrous auburn hair. "We don't give out the names of our guests. You may call the operator and ask to be connected to your party." She indicated a phone on the wall across the lobby.

At this point I realized how impetuous I'd been. What was I to say if I called and he actually answered? I felt like a star-crazed teenager. It was only a book after all. I thanked the woman and went outside. As I ambled back to the café I thought how silly I'd been. It probably wasn't Cortázar. What were the chances? I sat down at the table where I'd been sitting before and read a few more pages of my book. But the notion kept nagging me: if it was Julio Cortázar and if I waited in the lobby, I might get to meet him.

I didn't have anything else to do, so I went back to his hotel and seated myself in a deep brocade armchair that commanded a strategic view of the lobby. Sooner or later, whoever he was, he would come out. It didn't take long. The same man stepped from the elevator and turned to go into the bar. I drummed up my nerve and followed him inside.

He was sitting on a stool, the only customer at a long, varnished bar. He had already given his order to the bartender, who was mixing a scotch and soda. A pack of Gauloises rested on the counter beside an ashtray. I sat down next to him and ordered what he was having.

From the boldness of my move he must have thought I was a hustler making a pass. He glanced at me out of the corner of his eye and, unprompted, said he was waiting for his girlfriend to join him.

"Excuse me," I said, "aren't you Julio Cortázar?"

"No. My name's Robertson. Englishman."

He wasn't fooling me. He spoke with a distinctive accent, part French, part Spanish. I attributed his deception to a desire for privacy. I placed my book on the bar with his dust-jacket photo facing up. He sniffed loudly but didn't say anything.

"I admire your work," I said.

"Do you?" He seemed surprised and pleased at the same time, as if he didn't expect an American to know his work. "Whose? Mine or Cortázar's?"

"Yes."

He drew deeply on his cigarette, nodding at his amused reflection in the mirrored wall of bottles facing us. Finally, he said: "May I ask, have you ever read 'Las babas del diablo'?...They called it 'Blow-Up' in English."

"Of course."

"Did you like it?"

"Very much."

"And did you ever see the film?" Pronouncing it "feelm."

"You mean Antonioni's?"

His dark eyes focused on mine as if to inquire if there were any other. "What did you think of it?" he asked.

Until that moment I'd never given it much thought. It was just a movie after all, one I'd seen on a high-school date with a girl named Jane Johansson when all I cared about was if she was enjoying it enough that I might get lucky later. She didn't. I didn't. Now I had to think fast:

"Well, it wasn't the same really, was it?"

"Precisely."

The quickness of his affirmation gave me more confidence. "I mean, the movie was set in London instead of Paris. And in the story the crime wasn't clearly a crime, although it might have become one."

"Exactly! The mendacity of perception and the veracity of the camera lens. That is why there were the clouds. In the film he invents this meaningless murder no one else sees. In the middle of a park no less. Ridiculous! And those mimes! Were there any mimes in the story?"

"But don't you think the mimes were effective? Especially at the end when they were playing tennis. It's one thing I remember vividly."

"There were no mimes in the story! Besides, the whole point was that the narrator was a translator, not a fashion photographer."

"It was?"

He shook his head in disgust as if to say "Stupid people!" He drew on his cigarette, lifted his chin, pursed his mouth and exhaled a stream of smoke over the bar. He snuffed out the cigarette stub, smearing black tar over the golden crest of the hotel on the ashtray. A minute went by. He seemed lost in thought, tapping his fingers on the bar. It was clearly jazz going through his head, crazy rhythms, possibly a Charlie Parker riff. He turned to me:

"You seem a reasonable person. May I confide in you?"

"Of course."

"I'm here on a mission of sabotage. 'Payback' I think you say in America." He turned to see my reaction. When I started to explain we use the word "sabotage" too, he raised his hand to stop me. He shifted his whole body toward mine and leaned closer, breathing cigarettes and scotch in my face. "I'm going to replace Michelangelo's script with my own. Let's see how he likes it when someone tampers with *his* artistic vision."

He leaned back, as if to capture my reaction from a wider angle.

"But how? I mean...there's got to be more than one copy."

"I've taken care of that. One by one I've been substituting them. Jack Nicholson left his copy in the hotel yesterday while he went out for a walk. When the maid was cleaning his room I slipped in and exchanged it. Pffft—easy! The last one is Michelangelo's personal copy."

This seemed so preposterous I suspected he was playing games with me, fabricating one of his stories on the fly. Enthralled, I played along.

"What's his movie about?"

"More stupidity! It's about a journalist who switches identities with a dead gun-runner to escape his past."

"Huh! And yours?"

"My story is much cleverer—does one say 'cleverer' or 'more clever'?" Before I could respond, he gave a Gallic shrug as if to say it didn't matter. "Mine is about a journalist who switches identities with a dead gun-runner to create his future."

"That's a pretty subtle difference."

"Perhaps, but critical. What is the point of switching identities if you remain the same person you were before?"

I pondered this for a moment, trying to decide if it was profound or ridiculous.

"But don't you think Michelangelo...uh...Mr. Antonioni will notice?"

"No, because—and this is so typical—it isn't even his story. An Englishman wrote it. Besides, in my version I have kept everything the same. Everything is identical except the ending."

"You changed the ending?"

"Yes, and no."

Now I was confused. "Then how will anyone know it's your script and not his?"

He smiled and blew a long jet of smoke into the air. "Because mine has a student driver in it."

"Pardon me?"

"Have you ever noticed how everywhere you drive in Spain you end up behind one of these damn student drivers going ten kilometers an hour? It drives me crazy." He smiled at the pun.

"If he can take a perfect story and put mimes in it, why can't I put a student driver in his lousy script?"

"You don't think he'll notice?"

"I told you. I rewrote the script so it is identical except for that. Besides, he has made the last scene so complicated, he'll be too busy to notice. I just need to replace his personal copy of the script. Will you help me?"

By now I was wondering whether I was talking to Julio Cortázar or a lunatic. If it was a game, it had gone far enough. "Sorry. I only came here to ask for your autograph."

"You know, in my script, as in the original, the gun-runner journalist meets a complete stranger who is the only person he can trust to help him pull off the switch. I guess that kind of thing only happens in films."

"I'm very sorry."

He shrugged and finished off the watery remains of his drink. "Very well. I understand. Please forget what we have discussed."

He stood up to go and with a frown of intense concentration snuffed out his fourth cigarette.

"Good luck," I said.

"*Au revoir.*"

After all that, I'd forgotten to get his autograph. Although, given my refusal to help, I wondered if he would have obliged. I finished my drink and left the bar.

The next day I read in the newspaper that Antonioni's crew was filming on Montjuïc then leaving Barcelona to shoot scenes in Andalucía. My encounter the day before with Cortázar (though it now crossed my mind he never actually *said* he was Julio Cortázar), seemed like a strange dream.

Several weeks went by. I gave the incident little more thought. Then, one afternoon as I was reading in my café (I had moved on to the Swedish crime writer Per Wahlöö whose books, censored by the Spanish government, could only be found on the black market), I saw the same man pass by again. Only he looked different. His hair was longer and he'd grown a beard.

Convinced it wasn't Julio Cortázar but someone playing a great hoax on me, one that my own enthusiasm had helped perpetrate, I decided to see what the man was up to. He moved briskly through the crowds on the street, headed toward the same hotel. I followed him inside and into the bar. He had already lit a cigarette. A fresh pack of Gauloises lay on the counter.

I sat down beside him.

"So! What are you doing here?" I asked, sounding more accusatory than I intended. "Antonioni is in Andalucía or Africa by now."

I expected him to finally admit his deception.

"Oh, it's you." He lifted a finger to draw the bartender's attention and ordered a scotch and soda. "I forgot to autograph your book." He rummaged in his jacket pocket, uncapped a fat fountain pen, reached for my copy of *The Lorry* and signed it without even noticing it wasn't one of his. I opened the book and read what he'd inscribed: "From one saboteur to another. —Julio Cortázar."

"I've just come back," he said.

"From where?"

"The coast. I completed my mission."

"Yeah, right!"

"You don't believe me?"

"I don't even believe you're Julio Cortázar."

"Fine."

We sat there sipping our drinks in awkward silence, staring at our images in the mirrored wall opposite until I couldn't take it any longer.

"You're telling me you stole Antonioni's script?"

"Not stole, substituted. It was easier than I thought." He took a long drag on his cigarette. "Michelangelo guards his jewels closely, but I had inside help. They were filming on the coast, staying in Marbella. Do you know Marbella?"

I shook my head.

"It's nice. Nice beaches. Nice casinos. I got to know one of his drivers—a young Mallorquín who frankly drinks too much. He told me things that helped me execute my plan. How Michelangelo carries his script in an aluminum briefcase. How each day at the shoot he always keeps it in sight. This driver also told me he had written copious notes on his master copy. That was an important detail. Copying his notes in longhand on the facsimile took some time and was essential to my success.

"Anyway, this driver had his own ideas about how a film should be made. He felt under-appreciated, so he quit. The next day I went out to the location and applied for his job. Fortunately, by this time my beard had grown out. I didn't want to run the risk of being recognized again. By the way, I'm thinking of keeping it. What do you think?"

I smiled and nodded. It looked good on him. He seemed pleased.

"I soon discovered everything the alcoholic Mallorquín had said was true. Michelangelo was becoming more and more dictatorial as shooting dragged on, demanding that scenes be redone if they weren't exactly the way he wanted. Naturally, they had fallen behind schedule. Each day, while the crew ate lunch, Michelangelo reviewed what still needed to be accomplished. No one dared talk if he was talking. I bided my time, always keeping an eye on the aluminum briefcase.

"Then one day we stopped for lunch at a seafood restaurant on the highway outside Almería. The crew was restless and irritated. It was hot and we had crowded into four vans to get there. Anxious about the work that needed to be done that afternoon, Michelangelo only allowed one beer per person. It was an unhappy meal. Everyone simply wanted to get back and finish the day's work.

"As we were leaving, Michelangelo and Jack Nicholson went to take a piss while we waited in the vans. When Jack returned, he hopped into the passenger seat where Michelangelo had sat before. Thinking Michelangelo was in the other van, we headed back to the shoot. When the last van showed up without him, everyone said, 'Oh shit!' We had forgotten the director! The funny thing is, no one wanted to go back to get him because that meant facing his wrath. Finally, we all decided to go."

He lit a cigarette and laughed softly as he extinguished the match.

"When we got there, Michelangelo was sitting alone at the head of our long row of tables. The waiters were stepping carefully around him, afraid to clear the plates and glasses. He was furious. 'To teach you all a lesson,' he said, 'I am going on strike for the rest of the day.' He handed me his briefcase and ordered me to take him back to the hotel.

"It was the opportunity I had been waiting for. While Michelangelo sulked in his room I took the script from the briefcase and copied his notes onto my version. It was perfect. You couldn't tell the difference. After I made the switch I told the others I'd had enough and was quitting. I left that evening."

He stroked his beard with satisfaction. "'Piece of cake,' I think you say."

It was too preposterous. I laughed and said, "Good story."

"You don't believe me."

"No. Sorry."

He smiled defiantly. "Then wait here." He slid off the stool, ordered another round of drinks and walked out of the bar. Several minutes went by. I began to wonder if he'd ditched me and stuck me with the tab. No sooner had this thought crossed my mind than he came back clutching a brown vinyl portfolio.

He unzipped the top and dropped a bound sheaf of paper onto the bar.

"What's this?"

"The script," he said haughtily.

I picked it up, feeling its bulk. The pages were dog-eared. Coffee stains ringed the green cardboard cover. "Which one?"

"The original, of course. Keep it. As a souvenir."

I opened the script to the title page:

Professione: Reporter (The Passenger)
Director: M Antonioni
Screenplay: M Peploe, P Wollen and M Antonioni
Production draft: 15 May 1974
RESTRICTED: Copy 1 of 24

Julio swallowed his drink, snuffed out his cigarette and picked up his Gauloises from the bar.

"Now, my skeptical friend, you must excuse me. Tomorrow I return to Paris early and I am very tired. So this is goodbye!"

I started to apologize but he cut me off. We shook hands and he left the bar. When I got up to leave, I discovered he had already paid my tab.

That night in my hotel room I read the annotated script. I'd never seen a screenplay before. Throughout, Antonioni's scrawled notes referred to camera angles, lighting and sound effects, actors' instructions, even minutiae about prop placement. I couldn't put it down and compulsively read to the end. There was no mention of a student driver in the last scene or anywhere in Antonioni's scribbles.

When finished I felt excited and dirty, as if I were an accomplice to a crime. I hid the script in the back of the desk drawer, worried that if someone discovered it, I might be arrested for theft. Unfortunately, a week later when I checked out of the hotel to return to the States, I forgot it was there. Or maybe subconsciously I meant to leave it. I do still have the Per Wahlöö book Julio autographed for me.

Recently I watched again that now famous ending of *The Passenger*. It would have been an amazing scene anyway, but Julio's intervention made it even better. Jack Nicholson is waiting for the gun-runner's next appointment, lying on the bed of a ground-floor hotel room in one of Andalucía's white towns. The tall French windows are open and the camera is positioned so you can see most of the room and through the wrought iron bars of the window. Outside is a dusty, bare, sun-baked plaza with the arched facade of an ancient bullring in the background and a patch of blue sky in the upper corner of the frame. The soundtrack is silent except for the natural sounds of daily life in a sleepy village—a hammer tapping on stone, a boy yelling to his friend, birds chirping, the whistle of a distant train, dogs barking.

Imperceptibly at first but steadily, the camera moves past Nicholson's legs toward the actions outside where an old man sits in the sun against the bullring wall calling to a stray dog and another man opens a faded red door to say something to the old man when—Julio's stroke of genius—the absurd little SEAT with a learning permit on its front grille and a driving school sign on its bulbous roof comes into view, inching across the plaza toward the camera before veering out of sight as Maria Schneider, Nicholson's girlfriend, wanders into the shot and takes a pensive look back at the hotel while a solo trumpet somewhere plays a paso doble as if someone were practicing for a bullfight, and then the SEAT lurches across the plaza in first gear going the other way, and still the camera draws slowly toward the barred window as a boy in a red shirt picks up a rock and throws it toward the old man, who scolds him, and a sleek cream-colored Citroën pulls up and the two bad guys get out, one of whom goes into the hotel while the other distracts Maria Schneider, leading her toward the bullring, as a woman in a bright red top and red running shoes jogs across the camera's view and you hear the tolling of church bells, doors closing, the murmur of voices in the hotel lobby, and—just as an abrasive two-stroke motorcycle engine revs—a bang that could be a muffled gunshot or an engine backfiring and the trumpet blows again, more doors shut and the bad guys drive away in the Citroën seconds before a toy-like siren wails and a green police car pulls up on the far side of the plaza, only to be surrounded by a crowd of excited children, at which point you realize the camera is no longer looking through the iron bars but has magically gone past them, as if it were Nicholson's soul freed to watch, as one policeman tells the children to scram while the other walks over to the parked SEAT and tells the driver to move along just as more police with Nicholson's wife race up in another car—too late of course—and they and Maria Schneider rush into the hotel and into Nicholson's room, which the camera is now facing, looking from the plaza through the iron bars, for the climactic moment when Nicholson's wife says she doesn't recognize the dead man but Maria Schneider says she does.

The camera cuts to a final wide-angle shot from the plaza. It's twilight and Julio's funny little SEAT with the *Auto Escuela Andalucía* sign starts its engine, turns on its headlights and drives a short way up the road and turns left out of the frame, leaving the camera's eye fixed on the stark white hotel, the desolate road, the distant hills, and a smoldering red sunset already half obscured by the cloud-filled darkness crushing the horizon.

Brilliant! And to think, for all these years no one but I knew we were watching Julio Cortázar's version of the movie. If you don't believe me, listen to Jack Nicholson's commentary on the DVD. He unwittingly confirms what Julio told me.

THE
RECRUITER

Mom's still pissed at me and Grampus. She blames him for me enlisting even though I told her I would've done it anyway. But she doesn't buy it.

Grampus comes to our house every Thanksgiving. He flies up from Phoenix and stays until the New Year. He likes being with us for the holidays, but the real reason he stays so long is the annual reunion they hold for his old unit at Ft. Lewis to celebrate the anniversary of the Battle of the Bulge.

His visits always stress my mom out. It's not like we have a lot of room or anything. Mom has to give up her sewing room, which is usually filled with bolts of cloth and half-finished church projects. When Grampus arrives none of those projects will get done even though it's the busiest time of year for the decorations and other stuff she likes to make. Still, she straightens up the room, pulls out the sofa bed and makes sure there's space in the closet for his things. But Grampus prefers to leave his suitcase open on top of her sewing table with his clothes in two piles, clean on the left side, dirty on the right.

"It's easier to find things," he says. There's no way she could really use her sewing machine. She just chalks it up to family.

While he's with us Grampus mostly hangs around the kitchen reading books or doing the crossword puzzle from the paper. Sometimes he'll take a walk around the neighborhood so he can have a smoke, since Mom won't let him smoke in the house. But it's not like he knows anyone up here, and there's nothing to see in Federal Way, especially in the winter when it's raining all the time, so he usually just sits around. At seventy-nine, I guess that's what you do wherever you are. In the mornings Mom's busy getting ready for work and she's always pressed to put something on the table for breakfast. "Here, let me," Grampus offers, but he doesn't really mean it, and Mom knows it. She'll fix him some toast and scrambled eggs, but if she's late she'll just get the cereal out of the cupboard and plunk the milk carton down in front of him. At night Grampus likes a glass of Jim Beam with water, no ice. He usually has a glass poured while he sits at the kitchen table. That way he can talk to Mom while she cooks. Mom just says "Uh-huh" like she's paying attention.

Not that she needs to. We've heard it all before. Mom tells me to be polite because he doesn't have anyone to talk to. But sometimes you just have to get away.

His stories are all about him, things that happened forty, fifty, even sixty years ago. His favorite subject is the war. It's like he's bought all that Tom Brokow greatest-generation crap lock, stock and barrel. How he enlisted in the Army straight out of high school in '43. How he wanted to fly P-51s but his eyesight wasn't good enough. "So much for the fighter pilot idea," he says. How he ended up in the infantry, trained in Texas, and eventually became a squad leader. "That's what Uncle Sam needed, so that's what they made me," he says.

* * * * *

It was while he was visiting last time that I decided to enlist, so you can't really blame Mom for seeing it the way she does. Ever since she and Dad split up, she's carried the brunt of things. She works until six, which means dinner isn't ready until seven, so after school Grampus and I would usually sit around watching TV. He never gets tired of watching CNN. We were watching when they caught Saddam Hussein in that hole in the ground. We must've seen that video a hundred times where they find the hole and then him looking all dope-eyed and wild-haired like some crazy homeless guy. I kept thinking, doesn't Grampus realize it's the same damn clip they're showing over and over? But he never got tired of it. He chuckled every time he saw it.

"Maybe next time he'll try to run away and they'll shoot him," I said.

Grampus smiled. "Want to watch something else?"

I shook my head. I didn't really care since I was playing my Gameboy.

We get along pretty good actually. It's because of me he's stuck with his name. When I was about four he visited us and was in a grumpy mood the entire time—I think it was right after Grammy died—and I asked my dad why he was being such a grampus. I'd meant to say sourpuss but somehow grampus came out. Everyone laughed and started calling him that and the name stuck.

"Aren't those guys something, Mikey!" he says, pointing to the screen. "Jeez, look at the damned equipment they have now! Like something out of Star Wars." He was admiring the camouflaged body armor worn by a soldier being interviewed by a reporter outside Baghdad, the padded, visored helmet and the two-way radio tucked into the breast pocket of his Kevlar vest. The guy looked really tense, like he'd been ordered to be nice to the reporter when what he was really thinking about was keeping his head down. You could hear shots popping in the background.

Grampus muted the TV with the remote and opened his book. Tom Clancy. Outside in the backyard it was raining lightly. There was a hummingbird on the feeder, a tough little guy who refused to go south for the winter. I was always telling Mom they'd go south if she stopped putting sugar water in the feeders, but she did it anyway.

"Look at that, Grampus." It was a male. You could tell because his head flickered iridescent crimson when he turned it.

"Huh?" He looked up, pushing those big aviator glasses he wears up onto the bridge of his nose. Maybe it's his age but Grampus always looks like he's frowning. You're never sure if he's pissed off or what. Now, looking at the bird, he just nodded vaguely as if he'd seen it before and once was enough. He went back to his book so I went to my room and listened to music.

That Sunday Manny, my best friend, asked me to help with a landscaping job he was doing for his dad. Hauling gravel and dirt in wheelbarrows to fill in around some new houses. I was dirty and soaked when I got home so I went straight to the shower.

When I came out, Grampus was in the living room sitting in the recliner with his feet up watching golf on TV. His book was nearly finished.

"Where's Mom?"

"Christmas shopping."

I took the bills from my jeans and smoothed them out on my knee.

Grampus looked up. "How much did you make?"

"Let's see. Twenty...forty...sixty-five bucks!"

"Is that good?"

"Good enough. I'm saving for an Xbox."

He smiled and stared at me.

"What?"

"So what are you planning to do when you get out of school? Play video games?"

I shrugged.

"Maybe you should join the service."

"Yeah, right!" Here it comes again, I'm thinking. More stories. He laughed like he'd read my mind.

"I was living on a farm in Wisconsin when the war started. I thought I knew a lot when I enlisted, but I didn't know shit, and the army made all the difference. Sometimes you need a good swift kick to get going."

"What's that supposed to mean?"

"Nothing. Just, sometimes it takes something outside of you to make things happen, that's all."

I've tried to explain to Mom that's kind of what happened to me. At school they have these monthly career days outside the cafeteria. Companies come in and set up tables: McDonalds, Starbucks, Home Depot. The Army's always there too. They tack up a big poster that shows soldiers leaping from a chopper hovering just above the ground, and they set up a couple of chin-up bars in front of it. The Sergeant, this guy named Murphy, knows most of the guys by name after being there so often and whenever we walk by he tries to get us to see how many chin-ups we can do.

"Cummings! Rodriguez!" he yells as Manny and I are walking past. "Ladke just did twenty. Think you can beat it?" Murphy is always wearing his camouflage uniform, combat boots and a black beret with an eagle on it. Except for the beret, you might mistake him for one of the guys at school. His face looks like a polished plate. Shaved red hair, a thick neck. He gives you this intense look like his eyes are drilling into you.

"Easy."

"Rodriguez," he says, "Take this dude down!"

The lunch line was long anyway so we took him up on it. Manny's your typical Mexican-American, short but solid as a rock, and real strong in the arms from all of the landscaping work he does, so we really went at it. I was on twenty-two and feeling it in my arms but Manny was right with me, matching me lift for lift. Murphy was giving both of us a hard time, saying wusses like us would never cut it in the Army.

At twenty-five Manny dropped to the ground. I pulled off one more and dropped, too. I think I could've done more but that was plenty.

"All right!" Murphy says, giving each of us a high five. "Gentlemen, the Army could use smart, good-looking stud stock like you." Always the sales guy he launches into his pitch. He's got his arm over my shoulder and has pulled Manny into the circle, leaning in close like he's going to tell a dirty joke. His breath is stale like he's on steroids or something.

"I mean, come on! What else you gonna do when you get out of here?" He nods toward the next table and winks, "Work at McDonald's?"

Manny's shaking his head. "Like I've told you, I'm going to work for my old man."

"Yeah, yeah. Landscaping, right? Well, that's okay if you want to do it. But in the Army you'd know you're making it on your own. I'm talking about mission-critical shit for your country. I'm talking about protecting basic values. And we offer a lot of benefits—"

"Yeah, like what? Shooting Iraqis?" Manny says, always the wise-ass.

But Murphy ignores him. "Full medical and dental, a college education if you want it, a cash sign-on bonus. We train you and get you started in real careers." He gives us a sly closing smile. "Think about it, that's all." Then, same as always, he shoves his business card into our hands, the one with the Army star in olive green. I must have thrown away a dozen of them.

For some reason at lunch that day Manny and I started talking about it for real. We were joking about who could do more chin-ups and got talking about what we were going to do after school. Truth is, neither of us had a clue. Manny liked to jerk Murphy around but he didn't really want to work for his old man. He'd already done it for four years. I wasn't sure what I was going to do. Forget college. I didn't have the grades or the money.

So it kind of started as a dare. Manny asked if I'd do it if he did, and I said maybe. We laughed at first but then we got serious. We knew it would freak our parents but the idea of putting our butts on the line for a change didn't seem like such a bad idea. I told Manny how Grampus had said his years in the army were some of the best in his life. Anyway, that's when we decided to enlist.

"Together all the way. Right, bro?" Manny said, and we shook on it.

We went back and told Murphy we'd meet him after school at the recruiting office in Tacoma. Instead, he offered to take us there himself.

He pulled up in a government-plated Ford Windstar. In the car Murphy talked about the commitment and what it meant. He wasn't being a sales guy now. He told us how it was hard work but worth it. Four years that went really fast compared to high school. He was already in his eighth year, he said, and loved every minute of it.

"You been to Iraq?" I asked him.

"Naw, not yet. Somebody has to stay and protect the homeland, right? Say, have you guys thought about what specialty you want to go into?" he asked. "Maybe you should consider electronic surveillance. It's becoming a big deal now. You like that idea?"

That sounded pretty sweet so Manny and I decided we'd list it as our first choice on the application.

When we got to the office, Murphy went through the paperwork, helping us fill in the things we weren't sure about.

"Do our parents need to sign?" Manny asked.

Murphy shook his head. "Not if you're eighteen. But it's always a good idea to discuss it with them. You've done that, right?"

We nodded.

"This is a big step, men. Sure you don't want to sleep on it?"

We shook our heads. We knew if we didn't go through with it then and there we might back down. We signed our names on the contracts and Murphy went to make copies. Manny laughed nervously. "My old man is going to flip," he whispered. I knew my mom would too, but I could hardly wait to tell Grampus.

Murphy came back smiling and handed each of us information packets. Then from the other side of the desk he leaned over and shook our hands.

"Congratulations, gentlemen, you are joining the finest fighting force in the universe."

"Shit, we joined the Marines?" Manny said, straight-faced. Murphy looked at him like his wise-ass days were soon over.

Well, Mom was even more furious than I expected. Murphy dropped us off at the school parking lot and Manny gave me a lift to my house. Grampus was still the only one home, sitting in his chair with the news on. He must've seen I was bursting.

"What's up, Mikey?"

"Promise you'll help me, okay, Grampus? Mom's going to be so pissed." I handed him the copy of my contract. Grampus pushed up his glasses to read it and whistled softly.

"No kidding."

When I broke the news at dinner Mom looked at me, then at Grampus.

"You what?"

I told her I'd be starting boot camp as soon as school was over.

"Over my dead body! You did this without discussing it with me? Does your father know?"

"Like he could give a rip."

"I don't believe this," she said.

"Mikey will be fine," Grampus said. "I'm proud of him."

"Was this your idea?" Mom asked, glaring across the table at Grampus.

Grampus shook his head, but I could tell she suspected otherwise.

"Well then, we're going down there tomorrow and tell them to forget it."

"You can't, sweetie. It's a contract," Grampus said.

"I don't care."

"The boy's eighteen. It's not the end of the world."

"Daddy, I'd appreciate it if you'd stay out of this."

The next weekend Mom was still mad and barely talking to either of us. On Saturday, she came into my room and told me I was going to take Grampus to his reunion whether I liked it or not. I made the mistake of saying, "Yes, ma'am," kind of quick. Without missing a beat she said I'd better get used to taking orders. She started to cry and left my room. I felt pretty bad.

At five Grampus was ready to go. He was in the living room all dressed up in his blue blazer. He'd pinned his medal ribbons to his chest pocket and, I have to admit, except for his goofy glasses, he looked pretty sharp.

"You mother will get over it," he said as we drove down the Interstate. A light rain was starting to fall so I put the wipers on. "She forgets, kids grow up."

"So, Grampus, why's it called the Battle of the Bulge anyway?" I asked to change the subject.

"Because the Germans were making a last-ditch effort to stop us before we crossed into Germany. In the Ardennes Forest they managed to push a couple of our divisions back, which created a big bulge in our front line."

"Where were you?"

"Below the bulge. Most of the time my unit was supporting the guys who'd been fighting since Normandy. They really knew their business. We'd only been in France a couple of months. But it could have been us in that pickle. A bunch of those units were as green as we were. They learned how to fight damn quick."

"Did you do any fighting? I mean, did you ever have to kill anyone?"

I'd asked him that question before but he'd always brushed me off with a scowl. Now, as I kept my eyes on the road, I sensed he wasn't annoyed. Maybe because I'd enlisted he figured I should have an answer, or maybe it was because we were headed to the reunion and his memories were stronger.

"No. At least none that I know of. Came close once."

I glanced over.

"During the battle?"

"Later. In a place called Alsace-Lorraine, near the German border. We were told to clear a village that was pretty much empty anyway. But they were worried about snipers so we had to go from house to house," Grampus began fishing for something in the inside pocket of his blazer. "Mind if I smoke?" he asked. He opened the window a crack and pushed in the lighter on the dashboard.

"There was this one brick house that looked perfectly fine except for a big hole on one side. You could see right into the second floor like it was a dollhouse. It was on an alley with a brick wall around it."

The lighter popped out and Grampus lit his cigarette, puffing a couple of times to get it going.

"Anyway, I went to check the house from the front, and my buddy, Howie Finchley—Finch we called him—went down the alley to check the back. When Finch turned the corner he found a German soldier with his back to him taking a leak against the wall. I think that German was as surprised to see Finch as Finch was to see him. He wasn't any older than us. Just a kid. No gun. No helmet. I don't know why he didn't just put his hands up. I mean, shit, your pants are unbuckled, a gun's pointed at you. I would've."

Grampus blew a long breath of smoke toward the crack in the window.

"Instead, he took a step toward Finch who couldn't tell what the guy was doing. Maybe he was trying to surrender or maybe he just panicked. Finch had his rifle pointed at him and the German reaches out with one hand and tries to take the end of it. Finch's yelling at him to back off and taking little steps back but the German won't stop. Finch was scared shitless. He didn't know what to do. He didn't want to shoot the guy but he sure wasn't going to let him get near either. By this time I was up on the second floor of the house watching this whole thing happen. I was about to shoot the guy myself, but Finch, well, he fired. Boom right into the guy's chest."

Grampus brushed an ash from his lap.

"By the time I got down to the ground, the German was dead with this twisted look on his face, a bloody hole in his chest, and his pants down around his thighs."

"Shit!"

"Poor old Finch was shook up pretty bad. I never have figured out what that kid was trying to do. I mean, the other times were completely different. Firing at some shadows moving in a grove of trees or across a river at some guys on the other side. You never really knew if you hit them or not. All you cared about was that they stopped firing back. But that time, that was something else. I still sometimes dream about it."

"Wow. Is Finch gonna be there tonight?"

Grampus frowned. "No. He died years ago. The war did a pretty good number on him."

We took the exit to the base and drove up to the main gate. Once the guard found out we were there for the reunion, he was really helpful, handing us a map and a parking pass. The reunion was in a modern brick hall near one of the old wooden barracks from the days when the cavalry still rode horses. Moist warm air that smelled of cooking hit my face as we entered. The room had a low ceiling and a linoleum floor like a cafeteria, but there was a stage at one end with a podium on it surrounded by flags: the American flag, the State of Washington flag, the US Army flag, the division's flag.

A bunch of round tables with white table cloths were set up for the banquet and in the back corners of the room a couple of bars with men crowded around them. A lot of Grampus's friends were already standing around the tables in the center of the room. They all looked pretty much the same, a bunch of geezers in white shirts and blue blazers. Some looked a lot older and frailer than Grampus and had brought family members along too. But they all seemed to be excited to be there.

A tall, thin guy with a silver mustache who Grampus said had been his company commander when he mustered out in '46 got up to the podium and asked everyone to take a seat. That took a while. The man welcomed everyone and said dinner would be in about a half hour. He said he wanted to get some business out of the way before everyone had more drinks and couldn't remember where they were. That got scattered laughter. Then he asked us all to stand to say the pledge of allegiance.

I don't know what I was expecting. I guess I figured they would talk about the war and remember the soldiers who died.

But it wasn't like that. After the pledge of allegiance, the guy at the podium requested a minute of silence for their fallen brothers. Everyone put their heads down. That felt pretty heavy. But then the room exploded with commotion. They all started getting up from their tables to greet friends across the room. They gathered in small groups to catch up on who'd died or who'd gotten divorced since the last reunion. They described their latest surgeries and accidents in excruciating detail. Grampus was right in there, with his glass of Jim Beam, proudly introducing me to everyone as his grandson who'd just enlisted. His voice grew animated as he told raunchy jokes to his buddies and ribbed them about their golf games. There wasn't any of the stuff we'd talked about on the ride down. Clearly these guys didn't want to hear it. They'd all been there. That's when I figured out why Grampus never missed these reunions. They weren't so much about honoring what they'd done or really even their friends who'd died. They were about the survivors, about surviving.

"Mikey, you want a beer?" my grandfather asked, squeezing my arm affectionately. His eyes were bright and his cheeks flushed with that healthy old-man pink after a drink. "No one here will mind."

"I can't, Grampus. I'm not old enough."

"Hell, if you're old enough to be a soldier, you're old enough to have a drink!"

"No thanks. Besides, I'm driving." But I was also thinking how much madder Mom would be if she found out.

TOO
LATE

As an undergraduate Peter Blackstone sometimes wondered what book he would be reading on the day he died. This seemingly morbid reflection had less to do with death than the affirmation of his chosen life as an academic, the fact he undoubtedly *would* be reading a book on the day he died. Death—especially his own—was hard to imagine except in an out-of-body way, like watching a movie of himself as an old man hunched in a chair in a garden with a blanket over his knees, and the book slipping from his lap as he gently succumbed.

As it happened, the book was Paul Fussell's *The Great War and Modern Memory*.

Published in 1975, Fussell's study of the war's impact on English literature won two national book awards. Fussell, a professor at Rutgers University, expressed surprise at the book's popular reception; after all, it was a work of literary criticism. But the subject seemed to touch the zeitgeist of the times (the demoralizing end of the Vietnam War), and to trigger an emotional acknowledgment of imminent loss, for the living memory of the Great War was rapidly fading. Soon, only written and photographic records, a few rusty artifacts and recollections told second-hand would remain. Fussell's book reminded readers of the need to comprehend this seminal event in their fathers' or grandfathers' lives before that generation was utterly gone.

As a graduate student at the University of Arizona, Peter chose the literature of war for his doctoral dissertation. For, as an ardent pacifist during the Vietnam War, he came to realize that all war literature is actually antiwar literature.

It was a controversial choice. His mentor felt war was an inappropriate subject for art and liked to quote a William Butler Yeats poem from 1915: "I think it better that in times like these a poet's mouth be silent..." Yeats, he said, pointedly excluded the Great War poets from *The Oxford Book of Modern Verse,* which he edited in 1936, arguing "passive suffering is not a theme for poetry. In all the great tragedies, tragedy is a joy to the man who dies; in Greece the tragic chorus danced."

How, Peter wondered, was war passive? Or tragedy a joy? In his thesis he asserted that war acts as an engine for art, much as it does for technology, and it defines each generation by adding new language to old while revitalizing timeworn imagery. From the siege of Troy, he contended, came a literary tradition that has shaped the telling of stories ever since and has been reshaped by every subsequent war.

Despite modest resistance from his dissertation panel, Peter defended his thesis successfully and received his Ph.D. in May 1975. The publication of Fussell's book that same spring may have validated his thesis, but it felled him in his tracks. After two years of research—reading, taking notes, outlining his arguments and tethering them with citations—Fussell had beaten him to the punch. Although Peter liked to think he might have written a book equal to Fussell's, it was too late. He might as well have wondered what poems and novels were never written by the millions of young men who died on the Western Front.

During his years at the university, Peter lived a frugal, focused life. The competitive intensity of the graduate program kept him invested in his studies to the detriment of much else. Then he met Margaret, whose finely chiseled chin, sharp nose and aloof posture reminded him of Katharine Hepburn. She was a graduate student one year behind him. They met in a seminar on D. H. Lawrence, for whom they shared a passion (she for the lyrical early novels that explored the sexual tensions between men and women; he for the later works that satirized the post-war impairment of Britain's upper class), and one passion led to another. They moved into a small bungalow together and argued about books and read to one another in bed. They spoke elliptically about getting married but agreed to focus on their degrees first.

Years later, Peter looked back on those days before his dissertation was finished, when he was working assiduously in his carrel at the library and Margaret was busy with poetry seminars and undergraduate writing labs—a time when the world seemed to revolve around the written word—and he felt an intense longing, a sense of regret that their lives had not stayed that way. Because of course they didn't.

With the aid of his mentor Peter received a temporary teaching position at the University of Wisconsin-Milwaukee, a job too good to turn down, while Margaret remained in Tucson to finish her degree. Before he left Arizona Peter considered proposing but decided it would be unfair to put that kind of pressure on her. Admittedly, he was also reluctant to assume such a commitment as he made his first foray into the world of work.

The job went well enough. He taught a survey course and inserted into the curriculum several books about war he hoped his young students would like: *A Farewell to Arms, Catch 22* and *Slaughterhouse-Five.* But his relationship with Margaret suffered from the distance, as if he were at the front and she were tending the home fire, which for him was the radiant gas heater in the bungalow that clanked on chilly nights when they would curl up together to read. He had difficulty explaining to her the politics within his department or the strange isolation he felt in the Midwest, especially as autumn turned to winter and the stairwell to his third-floor apartment filled with the sad smell of cabbage cooked by his landlady, a heavy-set Polish woman in her seventies who addressed him as Mister Professor.

He loved Margaret but was uncomfortable telling her outright. Instead, he used subtle code in letters or on the phone to communicate his feelings: "I miss you," or "I was thinking about you today," or "Tell me what you're reading." That winter, whenever he called, he sensed a growing distance in her voice. Again, he thought about proposing, but now he hesitated for a different reason: he was no longer sure she loved him.

Then, in late March—springtime in Arizona, where the cactuses and wildflowers bloom and the orange-like fragrance of sweet acacia drifts through classroom windows, but still the hardest part of winter in Wisconsin, where treacherous accretions of ice melt and refreeze under leaden skies and curbside snowbanks crystallize into crusty patches the color of soot—he received his "Dear John" letter (to use a wartime neologism). It was just like her to send one, to write down her thoughts rather than call him and possibly break into tears on the phone: "Dear Peter, I could put this in so many circumspect ways, but that would be unfair to you and dishonest. So here it is: I've met another man and fallen in love. It wasn't intentional; it just happened. I'm sorry."

His first impulse was to call her to plead his case, to tell her he loved her and missed her, to ask her to marry him. But, after reading the note several more times, he realized from its decisive tone it was too late.

Ten years later, there were still times when he thought about Margaret and wondered what their life might have been like together. He lost touch with her after a year but heard from a friend she was married and teaching women's studies in Florida. His own career had been patchy, with moves from one university to another as he filled associate positions without promise of tenure. He continued to write critical studies for the small scholarly journals read by his peers, but most were politely rejected. At one point, for about three years, he left the university setting entirely and worked as an editor at a publishing house in Chicago. There he met Julie, a secretary in the marketing department. In the beginning he often compared his relationship with Julie to the one he'd had with Margaret, which was grossly unfair because in memory he overlooked his many differences with Margaret and tended to minimize her ambition. But it was true, Julie didn't love books the way Margaret did or share the same interest in analyzing them the way he and Margaret had together.

Julie and Peter married in 1987 in a ceremony attended by a dozen friends in the chapel of a Presbyterian church in Oak Park. Not long after, he returned to teaching, this time at the University of Puget Sound, a small private college in Tacoma, Washington. The school didn't pay as well as the state universities but it placed less emphasis on publishing. There, he flourished, becoming a better teacher, and the teaching stimulated ideas for papers that, once again, he began to write and submit for publication.

Over the next twelve years Peter built a modest reputation for his expertise in war literature, a subject that rose and fell in popularity with each new conflict, whether it was one of the clandestine wars in Central America, the Gulf War, the civil wars in Somalia and Rwanda, or the Bosnian War and siege of Sarajevo (in which the same ethnic hatreds that ignited the Great War seemed to conflate again).

The resurgence of his reputation prompted him, when Oxford University Press announced the reissue of Fussell's book in a 25th Anniversary edition, to write a paper about the book's influence on the emergence of war literature as a legitimate field of study. He submitted an abstract to the Modern Language Association for its prestigious annual conference and it was accepted. Excited by the opportunity to argue the themes of his dusty dissertation to a wider audience, Peter took down from the shelf his dog-eared copy of Fussell's book to read again.

Around that time, in May 2000, he was digging up Julie's vegetable garden. Moles had invaded, destroying the roots of the pea vines—a kind of collateral damage in their foraging for grubs and worms. The pea vines were prospering and suddenly, just as they were about to blossom, they wilted and turned brown. Julie ruled out a virus in the soil; it was clearly the moles, whose tunnels could be seen running along the edges of the raised beds.

Peter decided to dig up the large timber-framed beds and replace the hardware cloth underneath. He had run the wire mesh along the bottom and tacked it to the timbers when he built the beds four years earlier. He suspected the original wire had rotted away, allowing the moles to infiltrate.

It was hard backbreaking work but Peter enjoyed it. He mounded the soil, heavy from spring rains, to one side as he cleared a section and scraped against the old wire mesh at the bottom with his spade. When he tugged at it his suspicions were confirmed. It broke away in pieces. After jabbing his hands multiple times, he cursed the moles, got a heavier pair of work gloves from the garage and resumed digging.

As he worked, he thought about Fussell's descriptions of the trenches along the Ypres Salient, a six-by-four-mile bulge in the front line protecting the old Flemish textile town. There, a million men were killed or wounded in four years of war. A million men in some twenty square miles—it seemed incomprehensible.

At first, the trenches were shallow, often no more than a few feet deep with the dirt mounded above. According to Fussell, the commanding officers never imagined the war would falter into one of stasis and attrition so, in their minds, there was no need for anything more substantial. The first battle of Ypres resulted in 24,000 British and 50,000 German dead, and did little but harden the lines of defense around the town. For the rest of the war, the Salient remained much as it was in 1914, with the British holding a virtually indefensible position (out of sheer pluck, said some; out of foolish pride, said others) and the Germans on three sides in possession of the high ground.

By the end of 1914, only five months into the war, the trench system around Ypres was fully developed. Good trenches zigzagged to avoid enfilade and were deep and lined with sandbags on both sides to protect from shrapnel. Dugouts and duckboard walkways kept men out of the weather and mud. Bad trenches, which were the majority near no man's land, ran like open sewers surrounded by the stench of rotting human and animal corpses.

But no trench, good or bad, offered much protection against the newest methods of warfare. In April 1915, for the first time ever, the Germans fired shells of chlorine gas at the Algerian and Canadian troops opposite them. Heavier than air, the greenish-yellow cloud seeped into the trenches, causing a burning sensation in the eyes, throats and lungs of soldiers whose only prophylactic was a dampened handkerchief. Those who did not suffocate immediately fled their positions, blinded and retching blood, and the Germans, wearing gas masks, swept in for the kill. British reserves barely managed to avoid a complete collapse of the line.

By the third year, the innovations of war took on a wholly new dimension. Fifty to a hundred feet underground, coal miners from the Midlands and Wales were digging tunnels across no man's land in order to place huge caches of explosive beneath the German lines. On the morning of June 7, 1917, after a three-week artillery barrage and moments before the troops went over the top, British sappers simultaneously detonated nineteen subterranean caches. The explosions, which were heard as far away as England, formed craters the size of lakes and instantly killed some ten thousand Germans, atomizing many and burying alive many more. The surprise was so complete, the British troops quickly captured Messines Ridge. Seven thousand dazed Germans surrendered; the rest fled in panic. Having gained so much territory, the Tommies had to halt their advance to rest and deal with prisoners. This delay allowed the Germans to regroup and dig in along their line of reserve trenches. Overwhelmed by success and overextended, the British abandoned their new position as indefensible and the Germans reclaimed the ridge. After three years of slaughter, the lines of the Salient remained unchanged.

Despite his admiration for the Great War's soldier-writers – Rupert Brooke, Robert Graves, Siegfried Sassoon, Wilfred Owen, Isaac Rosenberg and Edmund Blunden – Fussell argued they were not of the same caliber as their non-combatant contemporaries: Yeats, Pound, Eliot, Joyce, Lawrence and Woolf. They were not the innovators of their generation. To Peter, Fussell's assessment seemed harsh and unfair. That these young men managed to write anything was remarkable. After all, how does one humanize mass slaughter except through irony, the simplest forms and the plainest language?

By stripping away the artifices of art, isn't that too a kind of innovation?

As Peter dug in Julie's garden, his paper's theme played in his mind like a lively melody. He finished the garden repair after two days of hard labor. Julie admired the new beds with their dark lofted soil neatly raked into smooth mounds. She kissed him and expressed her excitement at being able to plant vegetables again. Peter nodded with satisfaction.

Three days later he began to write his introduction. His hand felt stiff but he dismissed it and soldiered on. He was simply feeling the repercussions of over-exertion; his arms and back ached from the workout, too. The stiffness in his hand subsided, but the next day he woke around five in the morning with an intense pain in his neck and shoulders, and he was having difficulty breathing.

Julie called 911 and they rushed him to the emergency room. Suspecting Parkinson's, the doctor placed him in the ICU and ran blood tests. The spasms intensified that afternoon, the muscles of his neck and back clenching of their own accord. The pain nearly made him lose consciousness. After giving him a muscle relaxant, the doctor, thinking it might be rabies, asked Julie if an animal had bitten Peter.

Toward evening a gray-haired Indian doctor with dark, sleep-deprived eyes, came on duty. He looked at Peter's chart and asked a few questions about his medical history and recent activities. The spasms were milder due to the relaxant but still lasted several minutes. Peter could barely attend to what Doctor Singh, who spoke with a thick accent in clipped bursts of medical terminology, was telling Julie.

Doctor Singh suspected tetanus and asked when Peter had received his last booster. Julie said she didn't know. It was several years since he'd seen a doctor, and because they'd moved several times and changed doctors in the process, the last booster may have been ten or even fifteen years earlier.

"Well," Doctor Singh said, "it's too late to give him one now. A booster's only good for preventing tetanus, not stopping it once it's in the body. What he needs now is TIG." Tetanus immune globulin, he clarified as he ordered the nurse to retrieve it from the hospital pharmacy.

While they waited for the nurse to return, Doctor Singh explained that tetanus is caused by a bacterium, Clostridium Tetani, which dies rapidly when exposed to heat or oxygen. But the bacterium produces a spore that is impervious to heat, oxygen and most antiseptics. These spores are common in soil, especially in barnyards and places where animals live, and in their manure.

"The problem," Doctor Singh said, "arises when the spores enter the body, typically through a puncture wound. They germinate in anaerobic conditions and as they germinate, they produce two toxins, one of which is so deadly it only requires 175 nanograms—that's 175 billionths of a gram—to be lethal."

Doctor Singh shook his head as if dismissing the layman's ability to conceive of such an infinitesimal amount.

"These toxins interfere with the body's neurotransmitters, which is why the spasms occur.

"This was entirely preventable," he said with a note of dismay.

Even in his battered state the doctor's next words caught Peter's attention. Doctor Singh told Julie the first passive immunizations, using antitoxins developed in animals, took place during World War I. "The efficacy"—a word Doctor Singh fired off—"of today's vaccine, which is made from human antibodies, was safely demonstrated during World War II. Unfortunately, since Peter's last booster was so long ago, these antibodies are no longer present in sufficient quantity to prevent C. Tetani from producing the toxin in his body.

"He needs the TIG right away," Doctor Singh said as the nurse returned. He administered the injection himself and, with a touch of pride, said it was fortunate he happened to be on call that evening. "Without immediate treatment the toxin is often fatal, and because immunization has made tetanus so rare, doctors are slow to diagnose it."

That evening Peter continued to have bouts of seizure marked by back-wrenching spasms that lasted several excruciating minutes during which he could only breathe in short painful gasps. Then he slipped into spells of exhausted peace when his mind cleared and he was able to recognize Julie, looking tired and anxious, in the chair across the room. He told her to go home and get some rest.

He drifted in and out of sleep despite the respirator attached to his nose. Although he had never experienced anything as painful as the spasms, he was comforted by Doctor Singh's quiet and self-assured manner. The doctor's frequent visits conveyed the seriousness of the situation but also the expectation that the illness was about to be broken. The tetanus was on the defensive. There was no unmasked terror of the kind the Great War's infantrymen must have felt as they waited for the whistles to blow, signaling the moment to go over the top. Peter's anxiety was more about enduring until the TIG took effect.

In the clear moments, Peter had flashes of insight into Fussell's book, which at his request Julie had brought from home and left on his bedside table. "Irony is the attendant of hope," wrote Fussell, "and the fuel of hope is innocence." Yes, thought Peter, as the Great War consumed innocence, irony served as inoculum, preserving hope amid the terrifying and absurd attrition. But as the adversaries developed new, more massive, more impersonal and deadly modes of warfare—as the toxin grew stronger—even irony proved inadequate. Was retreat into hopeless silence the only legitimate response? Was Yeats right after all?

Peter wished he had a piece of paper to write down his thoughts, but as he lifted his head to look across the room the respirator suddenly felt heavy and the oxygen tasted bitter, as if he were swallowing mustard gas. A violent, spine-shattering spasm sent the book flying to the floor. He tried to reach for the call button by his side but lost consciousness at the instant an explosion burst his eardrums and the darkness behind his eyelids atomized into an infinitude of white sparks.

AT
THE
WATER'S
EDGE

We descended the bluff to the beach. We walked slowly to the right then to the left as the asphalt path switched back and forth across the steep slope. I looked down at the thin strip of sand and the two stone jetties extending into the water. Between them, a connecting breakwater of jagged rocks lay half submerged like a shoal. Waves broke violently over the crumbling barrier. I didn't look but knew her eyes only followed her feet; her hand skipped nervously along the wooden railing. Leaning back, resisting gravity, we went as if pulled by some unkind fate. We didn't speak; we didn't touch.

The sky was a hollow glassy dome, the world encompassed by high gray cloud. The air felt damp and smelled of salt. As we neared the beach, the sound of waves and wind filled my ears. The windows of the building at the bottom of the path rattled in the wind; sand scratched at its closed door. The building looked empty but as we passed by I saw people inside playing cards at a table in a dimly lit room. It was early autumn, the beach deserted. I guessed they were concession workers straggling from the summer season.

The building was white but needed painting. Around the foundations sand had drifted and eaten away the stucco, exposing patches of concrete underneath. The walls were coated with salt hardened to a crusty glaze. On the building's cornice the red arrow of a broken thermometer pointed to 86 degrees. I imagined it sticking there on a summer day long ago, unnoticed by the children playing in the water or by the adults, radiant with sweat and lotion, dozing in the hot sun. It looked absurd now.

"You always go quiet," she said, looking at me then quickly looking away.

We sat down in the sand, which was damp from the ocean's spray and cold without sun. I looked up the bluff at the way we had come. The dry yellow grass rustled in the wind with a sound like someone sweeping. I couldn't answer her; there was a reason for bringing her here, but I didn't know how to tell her yet.

I surveyed the beach. It was empty except for an old man by the building and a young couple near the water. The man sat on a bench in the sheltered lee of the building. He leaned on a long-handled umbrella and his pant legs flapped whenever gusts curled around the corner. I had noticed when we passed that his jacket was too large for his frame and his flannel collar was frayed. An old tweed cap was pulled down to his ears. From beneath its brim he stared at the sea, the breaking waves. He didn't seem to notice us.

Her voice broke with the cracking of a wave against the shore:

"Damn it, Eric, can't you say something?"

"What do you want me to say?"

Her hair was blowing across her face. She looked down at the sand and dug her fingers in deep, coming up with fistfuls that slipped away. She was thinking.

My eyes drifted to the couple down the beach. The girl was skipping in the water, her pants soaked to her thighs. The boy walked along the shore close by, her sandals dangling from his hand. She reached down and splashed water at him but he dodged it. Then, laughing, she peeled off her sweater, tossed it toward him and fell back into the water. I winced, imagining the cold closing over her, but she swam with ease. The boy lay back in the sand, propped on his elbows, watching.

"You always say that. How can I tell you what to say?" The muscles of her face pulled and contracted as she wrestled with her words. "Whenever I ask you for anything, you can't seem to give it. I can't..."

She polished a thin black pebble with her thumb.

I looked out at the ocean—grays and greens flecked with white. The sky and water blurred into one at an indistinct point. The girl was still swimming. She floated on her back, waving to the boy, trying to entice him in. I watched her body rise as the waves swelled and surged past her. She stroked to recover ground, gradually working her way to where the waves were breaking. "Eric, look at me."

I looked. She was starting to cry.

"Oh...I didn't want to cry. I'm not going to cry this time." She wiped her eyes with her sleeve.

"What is it, Eric? Lately I've needed you close to me and you haven't been there. Everything's for yourself." Her gaze fell from me to the sand. "Why can't you make me feel you love me? Why can't you just touch me? Even in bed—" she punched the sand, "even in bed you don't want to touch me anymore."

"Stop it, Sarah."

I closed my eyes and leaned back. It felt as if the sand were giving way underneath me, burying me. The fighting had become like sand crushing my chest.

I sat up and our eyes met; it was as if she knew what I was about to say. I looked down the beach at the old man on his bench, at the boy lying in the sand, at the girl tossed by one wave and slipping beneath the next. I counted the seconds, one...two...three, waiting for her to emerge. Four...five...six. I got to my feet. The boy was already running toward the water. He checked himself to pull off his shoes. Waving frantically with both arms, he shouted for help. Then he dove into the water.

I reached the water's edge out of breath and without realizing ran into the cold surf up to my knees. There was no sign of the girl and I found myself wishing the sea would stop moving altogether. The boy swam with a clumsy stroke, slapping the oncoming waves like an exhausted boxer. Finally he reached the spot near the breakwater where she had gone under. Four times he dove, and each time I expected him to disappear. By now the workers from the building had gathered and I could hear their voices behind me—

"What happened?"

"Call 911."

"Where is he?"

"Oh God!"

Until I heard her voice, I didn't realize Sarah was standing beside me, her fist clenched and pressed against her mouth. I looked back across the water and saw the boy surface again. He stroked with one arm, struggling to keep the girl's head above the water. When he came closer to shore another man and I helped carry her to the beach. Blood streaked from a gash on her forehead. Her T-shirt was torn. Her arm was slippery in my clutch. The boy staggered up to us on the arm of another man. He was breathless and blubbering. Sarah wrapped him in a jacket someone handed her.

The man who had helped me carry the girl ashore was kneeling over her trying to revive her. The girl's lips were blue, her cheeks white. Viscous green water came from her nose and mouth as the man pumped with both hands on her chest, counting out loud with each stroke. But she would not breathe. He pressed his mouth to hers, pinched her nose and blew air into her lungs. Still she would not breathe. The color refused to return to her face. The boy was crying, shivering now with cold and shock. "She must," he implored, "she must, she must!" With growing urgency the man again counted and pushed the palms of his hands against her breastbone, then he tilted her head back to continue artificial respiration.

Kneeling beside her, I held the girl's cold hand in mine. The man trying to resuscitate her stopped, shook his head, and wiped his mouth in frustration. Above us a siren's oscillation came to an abrupt halt as a fire truck arrived at the top of the bluff.

All this time the old man had been standing to one side. Now he approached and bent down to peer at the girl. He reached out with a gaunt hand and gently tried to brush the wet sand from her cheek. "So young!" he said, softly. "What a terrible thing." He stared at the dripping, shaking boy standing opposite him. He seemed about to say something but instead unhooked the handle of the umbrella from his arm and used it to balance himself. He turned to me and with a sad smile said, "Your friend will hurt a long time." I was about to explain that I didn't know the boy, but the old man had turned and was walking away. He moved slowly, leaning on the umbrella, his leather shoes slipping in the soft sand. I took Sarah's hand and we followed him as if he pulled our souls along. I let the noise of the wind and waves dull my thoughts. I let them wash my voice away.

THE
MAN
DIED

The man died.

That was my story—beginning, middle and end. It said all I wanted to say. I thought about it long and hard and decided it was the story I had to tell.

It was the end of the semester and I needed to turn something in if I didn't want to flunk.

"That's it?" my creative writing teacher asked. Blue eyes narrowing, incredulous smile widening. He turned the page over as if it were a joke. Baffled amusement behind the reddish-gray beard.

"That's it," I said.

"Bullshit," he said.

"Why do you say that?"

"You think you're going to submit a single, three-word sentence and get away with it?" He laughed as if it must be a joke. "I've seen plenty of BS'ers, Baxter, but this takes the cake. You've got some nerve, I'll say that for you."

I stood there while others turned in their assignments. Loud dudes with their hats on backwards casually tossed their manuscripts on the desk. Girls with cell phones provocatively wedged in their waistbands handed their stories to him and coyly warned they weren't as good as they'd hoped.

"What do you mean?" I asked.

"The man died," he said, quoting. "That's it?"

"Yeah."

"Get serious, Baxter. What man? What did he die of? When? Where?"

In a way his questions were an acknowledgement that my submission wasn't a joke, and for that I felt they deserved consideration.

"Does it matter?" I asked.

"Of course it matters! Here–" He handed me my story. "Go figure it out."

I took the paper and asked when he wanted it back.

"By the end of the week," he said, shaking his head. "Or I'll have to give you a failing grade."

I left the classroom. I didn't think it was necessary to know what the man died of, but clearly my teacher did. So I gave it more thought, and the more I thought the more possibilities came to mind, countless images from television and the movies.

There was death by gunshot, death by swordplay, death by auto accident. Death by hanging, electrocution, lethal injection. Death by strangulation or beheading. There was freezing to death, starving to death, dehydration, drowning, suffocation, sunstroke. Death going under the knife, over the top, down in flames, up in smoke. Hit and run. Hit man. Influenza, pneumonia, Ebola, plague. AIDS, SIDS, SARS. Cirrhosis. Suicide. Suicide bombing. Hara-kiri, kamikaze, carbon monoxide, cyanide. An overdose of pills, coke, heroin, crack. Cancer, stroke.

I marveled at the ways writers sit at their desks and kill off characters. The options seemed endless. But I had considered each of these when I wrote my story and rejected them all.

"Write what you know," our teacher said on the first day of class.

How many men had I seen die? Only one. My father, the month before, of congestive heart failure. Actually, I didn't see him die. He died in Tucson and I was in Seattle. But I had seen the approach of death when I visited him after his heart attack. The blue-gray circles like bruises sloughing from his eyes. The flaccid, unshaven cheeks. The oxygen tank and long spiral of plastic tubing leading to a clear latex mask that he sucked on while he sat on the family-room couch dressed in his navy-blue bathrobe, striped pajamas and leather slippers watching daytime TV–CNN or the People's Court or the Weather Channel. It was as if he were inhaling a narcotic. Five deep breaths, five short ones. Five deep, five short. Then he could remove the mask for a while and pretend things were normal again. Do a crossword puzzle or watch TV as if it mattered. Judge Judy finds for the plaintiff three hundred dollars. What's nine letters for what Mr. Kurtz said?

My brother was there when he died.

"I'm having a hard time breathing," my dad said. "Maybe we should go to the hospital."

"Are you sure, Ed?" my mom asked.

"Yes, pretty sure," my dad said between labored breaths.

"Andy, help your father to the car," my mom said. "I'll call the hospital and let them know we're coming."

My dad was already up, heading through the kitchen toward the carport, dragging the wheeled oxygen tank behind him until Andy was able to pry its handle from his grip. Walking at first but then his walk turned into a terrified trot and would have become a run if he could have gotten free of the plastic tether and cylindrical anchor. He would have done a dash as if it were only fifty yards to the hospital and he were eighteen years old again. Because even with the oxygen he couldn't breathe enough air into his lungs and all of a sudden his heart must have felt like a chicken gizzard exploding in the microwave.

My dad collapsed on the carport floor. He'd almost made it to the car. Andy tried to give him mouth to mouth, but he didn't really know what to do except for what he'd seen on TV. He knew he should check his airway for a blockage in case my dad was chewing gum or had swallowed his tongue. He wasn't sure if he should be pressing on his chest but figured that was for drowning victims. He'd never seen someone die before either. Definitely not a sixty-year-old man in his bathrobe and pajamas on the carport floor beside the open door of an old Mazda with his head pillowed on his jacket.

By the time the paramedics got there my dad was gone or nearly. He wasn't really breathing. Andy said my dad shuddered, his back arched, his eyes bulged and his chest swelled with one last panicked gasp. Then, for what seemed like minutes but may have only been seconds, there was a slow, steady rattle in his throat like phlegm clearing.

The paramedics must have watched a lot of TV too, *Highway to Heaven* reruns or something like that, because the medic who took over felt for a pulse, asked Andy for my dad's name, then leaned over and shouted into my dad's ear as if he were deaf and not unconscious: "It's okay, Ed. Go to the light. Go to the light, Ed."

At least that's what Andy said he said.

I think about my dad being told this by the paramedic. My dad was not a religious man. By nature he was a skeptic. He raised us to observe the world and draw our own conclusions. While he was in the hospital he asked me if I believed in an afterlife. I didn't know what to answer, afraid if I said I did, he would think I was placating him, and if I said I didn't, fear would overwhelm him.

"Who knows?" I think I finally said.

My dad's eyes were green, a pale sea green like mine, and whenever I tried to slip a fast one by him, he would give me a stern look, point to his eye and ask, "Do you see any green in my eye?" It was his gentle way of telling me he wasn't fooled. In the hospital, as I answered him, I half expected him to lift his index finger to his eye.

"This scares the hell out of me," he said instead.

He looked shrunken and weak. He was not afraid to admit his fear. It was his love he had such a hard time expressing, saying out loud what I knew he clutched in his failing heart. I must have gotten that trait from him too, for I didn't tell him then, when I could have, for fear of what it meant—the unthinkable finality of it—that I loved him. I could have, but I didn't. Not then, not later.

"The best writers write their truth," my teacher likes to say. "Be honest."

The man died. That was what happened. He could flunk me if he wanted.

ABOUT THE AUTHOR

Tom Gething was born and raised in Milwaukee, Wisconsin. He studied English literature at the University of Arizona and received an MBA from the Thunderbird School of Global Management. He is the author of *Under a False Flag*, a novel about the 1973 coup d'état in Chile.